DON'T CROSS THIS LINE

DON'T CROSS THIS LINE

THE KURTHERIAN GAMBIT™ BOOK 14

MICHAEL ANDERLE

DISRUPTIVE IMAGINATION®

LMBPN Publishing
PMB 196, 2540 South Maryland Pkwy
Las Vegas, NV 89109

Version 2.53 February 2023
eBook ISBN: 978-1-68500-042-4
Print ISBN: 978-1-64202-052-6

DON'T CROSS THIS LINE TEAM

Beta Editor / Readers
Bree Buras (Aussie Awesomeness)
Tom Dickerson (The man)
Sf Forbes (oh yeah!)
Dorene Johnson (US Navy (Ret) & DD)
Dorothy Lloyd (Teach you to ask...Teacher!)
T S (Scott) Paul (Author)
Diane Velasquez (Chinchilla lady & DD)

Thanks to our JIT Readers for this Version
Brent Bakken
Heath Felps
Andrew Haynes
Kelli Orr
Gage Ostrander
Leo Roars
Hari Rothsteni
Björn Schmidt

**Thank you to the following Special Consultants
for DON'T CROSS THIS LINE**

**Jeff Morris - US Army - Asst Professor Cyber-Warfare,
Nuclear Munitions (Active)
Heath Felps - US Navy CPO (Active)**

Editor
Lynne Stiegler

*To Family, Friends and
Those Who Love
To Read.
May We All Enjoy Grace
To Live The Life We Are
Called.*

PROLOGUE

<u>Meeting Room, QBS *ArchAngel*</u>

"Fuck them," she whispered into the silence.

The men and women in the QBS *ArchAngel* didn't breathe, didn't flinch.

Their Queen was speaking.

Bethany Anne turned toward her people. She had been gazing at the giant screen showing Earth hanging in the expanse of space beneath them. Her eyes narrowed, glowing red, her lips compressed. "They have attacked us for three solid years. They have hunted people only tangentially connected to me through companies I no longer own." She looked around at the faces of those watching her. "They have attacked some of your families, and I have tried to be understanding. To offer the other cheek."

Bethany Anne twisted her head left, then right. Her vertebrae popped loudly in the room's silence both times.

She continued, "We have taken care of terrorists and saved people and countries from evil men and women in the night, and we've never asked for accolades, support, or even a fucking 'thank you.'" Her voice turned to ice, cutting through the room. "They keep pushing and pushing and pushing." She paused a moment and exhaled. "I've tried being civil." Her eyes flashed red as she whispered, "No. More."

"ADAM!" Bethany Anne snapped.

"Yes?" His voice came through the large room's speakers.

Bethany Anne looked up slightly. "Push the command out to my people. We aren't taking any more shit from anyone on Earth. The Etheric Empire has officially fucking had enough, thank you very much."

Bethany Anne nodded sharply and started walking crisply toward the door. "Admiral Thomas?" she called. His acknowledgment was immediate. She continued, "Make sure the captains of the fleet know that weapons are hot. I'm not taking another bullshit move like they just pulled. Any country tries that again, we level something important. Got that?"

"Yes, ma'am," Admiral Thomas replied as she exited the room.

Admiral Thomas' left hand clicked a button on his lapel as he started walking toward the door. "Admiral Thomas to all captains. Weapons are hot. I repeat, *weapons are hot.*"

The men and women in the room filed out behind their Queen.

She had tried to take into account what drove those on Earth, but no one had understood that Bethany Anne's reactions to the attacks against her and her people had been substantially restrained.

Now the gloves were coming off.

Author's Notes, Frank Kurns' Stories of the UnknownWorld: The Time of Patience

My name—my full name—is Franklyn Adam Kurns, and I am over one hundred years old. I have seen more shit in my life than any human could be expected to behold and stay sane.

I started out in the military before going into a covert organization to help hide the reality that there were others living among us who were the real monsters in the night.

I used my position to help one group of these monsters—or so I thought them—against another. You see, at that time I thought our folklore about vampires and werewolves was real. I had no idea at the time we were all human.

Just, some humans had been subjected to advanced genetic modifications, often accompanied by a very hot temper.

The Time of Patience, the series of books I'm going to release with other authors, took place during the last three years. The years since the big dustup in the Antarctic.

I'm sure you've heard about it.

Depending on who you listen to, TQB was down in Antarctica stealing old Nazi technology, or we attacked the US Navy (we did not, we protected them no thanks to the ungrateful asses in the brass) or we were working on communicating with aliens to take over the world. (Seriously? Who comes up with this shit?)

We have tried to stay off the world's radar for the last three years, the reason being that we needed to build our own house, so to speak. One of them is inside an asteroid, so it *is* kind of large.

We need all the technology and ships to protect the Earth against aliens, aliens who want to come and subjugate mankind. That whole story of us bringing aliens to Earth is complete lunacy.

During the Time of Patience we visited Earth pretty often, but rarely did you hear anything about it since we stayed out of the news to the best of our ability. We only made the news when our Academy students went off the reservation, just like any kids in any country since…ever.

I'll have a few books out about that soon enough.

I will upload these final books before we traverse the Yollins' annex gate.

Unfortunately there were those on Earth who continuously

pushed Bethany Anne and struck at us, but for the last three years she has not fought back as the attacks warranted. Apparently that caused them to believe our Queen was weak and unwilling to fight.

A toothless nag, some thought her.

Now, I am sure most people are aware of just how wrong that supposition truly was, but so you can see both sides of the story, I'm going to relate what happened before the chaos and the carnage.

Believe whichever side you wish. I have attached the video proof that goes with my assertions. Further, I will include supporting documentation—WikiLeaks style—that supports the videos.

I suspect a lot of this will be quashed, since very powerful people would not wish this information to be in the public domain. I hope others copy the data and keep it as a living testament against the powerful elite who believe the common man lacks common sense and is incapable of seeing the self-centered bullshit they pull.

What you do with the information I provide I leave to you, but I hope that my trust in the basic righteousness of humanity is deserved.

Now for the events leading up to the divorce...

Ad aeternitatem,

Franklyn Adam Kurns

T-minus forty-eight hours before we cross the line.

CHAPTER ONE

<u>Dulce Lake, New Mexico, USA</u>

Patrick Brown, the principal overseer of the operations side of Majestic 12, nodded to Dr. Eva Hocks when the two of them met in front of the elevator that went down to floor two-six.

Usually the good doctor and Patrick would trade jibes with each other, but never on quarterly meeting day.

"I hate this," she whispered to him as they both turned their keys and punched the separate buttons for the elevator to come up and get them.

Patrick kept his voice low. "This time, Eva, I'm completely in agreement. Whatever benefits we gain from the technological advances is certainly offset by having to deal with *them*." He nodded at the elevator doors, which were still closed.

Eva breathed in as the elevator arrived and the doors opened. Both wrinkled their noses as the smell from Section Two wafted up the elevator shaft. It was unpleasant and slightly nasty.

It was alien, Patrick decided.

Patrick waved his hand for Eva to go first, and she rolled her eyes. "Sure, be a gentleman when we enter the elevator to go down to the belly of the beast, why don't you?"

Patrick stepped in behind her and slid his key in, turning it before punching in the code to go down.

The doors closed.

"Well," he began as they descended the two hundred feet. "I don't mind being a gentleman, but that puts me into specimen category with you. I figured out a while back that 'specimen' was a bad situation where you're concerned."

"Is that why you are always a pain in the ass?" Eva looked at him, not sure if Patrick was giving her a hard time again or being honest.

"Um." He paused before shrugging. "That's probably truer than I care to admit, really." He didn't return her look.

Interesting, she thought, *he seems uncomfortable. I wonder what else causes this to occur?*

"You're doing it again," he stated flatly.

"What?"

"You're studying me again." This time he did look at her, annoyance written on his face.

Eva closed her eyes. "You can take the scientist out of the lab…"

The elevator stopped and the doors opened as Patrick finished the phrase, "But you can't take the lab out of the scientist." This time he stepped forward in an ungentlemanly way and asked over his shoulder, "What the hell is that supposed to mean?"

Patrick stopped and waited just long enough for Eva to catch up before resuming. "I mean, I get when you say you can take the guy out of the fight but not the fight out of the guy or something similar, but a lab?"

Eva shrugged, desiring to chat even less as they went farther into level two-six.

"Lord, I hope we don't have to speak with Ztopik." Patrick looked behind them, talking softly. "The little guys are bad enough, but looking up into his pink eyes just freaks me the fuck out."

"Would you please," Eva hissed, "not speak about him down here?" Patrick pursed his lips and nodded. After another two minutes of walking down the smooth rock hall, Patrick and Eva came to a door. The portal was a little taller than most human doors would be.

Patrick nodded to the two three-and-a-half-foot-tall gray aliens beside the door. Neither wore anything but a holster for their small weapon, which looked like a black flashlight with three small buttons. Each button altered the level of destruction.

Set to level one, the guns sucked. Level three buttons, max, supposedly wiped your atoms from existence. Fortunately or unfortunately, the little guys didn't have much in the way of self-awareness. Most Grays were mind-bonded to a superior, and to date Patrick had only met one superior.

They pushed the door open and inside the ten-foot room, walls and ceiling painted white, stood Ztopik.

Eva pushed down her anxiety and smiled cordially, even if Ztopik's pink eyes always caused her confusion. She thought of bunny rabbits with piranha teeth whenever they came down and had their quarterlies with him or his delegate, although he had no teeth that she had ever been able to discern in the small slit of a mouth that graced his face.

"Welcome, Patrick, Overseer, and Eva, Lead Scientist." He was over seven feet tall and his thin body barely had enough shoulders to drape the silvery robe over without it sliding off.

"Hello, Ztopik. How do the studies go?" Patrick asked as he and Eva took two chairs around a white table, leaving the modified seat for Ztopik to use when he chose to sit down.

"As always, effectively if more slowly than I would prefer," he replied in his musical voice. Ztopik waited for them to sit before he pulled out the last chair and sat as well, adjusting his robe underneath himself. He looked back at the two humans, his eyes never blinking. "I understand that there are happenings on the surface?"

Oh shit, Patrick thought. He had hoped to keep everything about TQB from Ztopik. There had been a critical incident in 1979 in these two levels that had killed hundreds of people. Killed them easily, in fact. Patrick's job was a delicate balance of allowing necessary evil to occur to acquire the needed technologies from Ztopik and his people down here in these levels.

"There are always happenings, but which one are you asking about?" Eva interrupted, her voice cracking. Ztopik ignored her vocal weaknesses; he was amused by how much she feared these meetings. Fear was the ultimate indication you were a slave, not a master.

Ztopik feared nothing on this planet.

"I understand that the humans who expressed they were in communications with aliens almost a hundred of your years ago have been communicating with outside emissaries at this time?" The hairless white face turned back and forth between the two humans.

"Yessss," Patrick agreed, drawing out his answer to give himself time to think about where Ztopik was going with this.

"I want one of your people in the meeting," the alien finished.

"Why? Isn't that dangerous?" Eva asked, her curiosity driving her fear to the side.

Ztopik turned and stared at Eva for a moment, prolonging the silence. The little power play irritated Patrick, but he and Eva had argued about her fear for years and it got him nowhere with her. Ztopik liked to tweak Eva.

Maybe it gave him an alien version of a hard on. Who could say?

Eva mumbled something unintelligible and Ztopik turned his head slightly before answering, "No, we have the ability to block Dr. Abesemmins' memory of this location, and give him a proper cover story, given time."

"You want Abesemmins to go?" Patrick blurted out. Of all the members of the human team, Abesemmins was the least likely to want to.

"Of course," Ztopik answered Patrick. "He has a good cover, correct?"

"Well, yes," Hell, they all had good covers with the government.

"My people will protect his mind and give instructions on what we wish to know from those who provided the technology. We shall determine if anyone here on this world has given her the information she has."

"What people?" Patrick was confused. As far as he knew, Ztopik was the only leader. He wasn't aware of other aliens like Ztopik on Earth. Patrick wasn't even sure if Ztopik was a proper emissary, or represented his race's version of a splinter group. If there were more of his kind here on Earth, that might be a problem.

"That is not known at this moment, Overseer Patrick."

Ahhhh, shit. Ztopik was using his title now. That was equivalent to a parent saying a child's full name.

"Okay. How can we help?" Patrick asked.

"I thought this was obvious?" Ztopik answered. "I wish Dr. Abesemmins to come down here, and then go on this trip with the American government to Schwabenland to speak with Maria Orsitsch. He will ask certain questions, and depending on how she replies, I will know if we have a problem."

"What problem?" Eva blurted out.

Patrick raised an eyebrow. What had her on edge?

"A name that will mean nothing to you, Dr. Eva Hocks."

"Perhaps, perhaps not," Patrick temporized, trying to get Ztopik's attention away from Eva. Her interruptions were annoying him; they were like a cat that was disgusted with a mouse trying to fight instead of fleeing.

"Go on, Overseer Patrick."

"We hear a lot in all sorts of circles. Perhaps if we knew this name, we would either recognize it or tell our people and our contacts to listen for it?"

Ztopik considered that, then slightly lowered his head on his fragile looking neck. "You make a good point, Patrick. The name you and your team should be listening or looking for..." Ztopik's eyes, which generally never gave indication of any emotion, seemed to flash red as if a super-fast wave had crossed them and then cleared back to his usual pink.

"Is 'Kurtherian.'"

New York City, New York, USA

Tabitha hunched her shoulders in her coat. She didn't need it for warmth, but rather to cover the weapons and Bat-shit she had hidden around her body.

She could just kill Bobcat and William. Those motherfuckers had stolen into the Tontos' rooms and drunk beer and watched the Batman movie starring Michael Keaton, then they followed it up with the Christian Bale version and got to talking about all the wonderful toys Batman had.

Then they damn near whispered how Tabitha's little toys and Batman's toys were kind of the same, weren't they? So now Tabitha had Bat-toys. Even Jean Dukes would ask her about her toys when she went to ask about another weapon or weapon idea.

She was so going to grab them by the balls and lift them into the air as they sang like the sopranos they needed to be. Didn't they realize this Bat-toy shit was going to last for decades?

God, vampires didn't forget anything. It was like they savored every little fucking joke *forever*.

Her watch thumped against her wrist and Tabitha took a left down a narrow street that looked like it cut across to the hotel she and the team were staying in. It was getting dark sooner now, and the chill autumn winds swept through the street.

If Bethany Anne didn't need Bobcat and William so badly she would...

"*Ay, mami, tù tan caliente!*" a man called from in front of her, followed by a couple of hoots. Tabitha focused ahead instead of on her feet, fuming at those two irritants, and could see five guys coming at her from the intersection ahead. She rolled her eyes. She didn't have time for this shit, but felt a need to do it anyway. She looked around and smiled. Across the street was a dark, dank, and smelly alley.

Perfect!

She couldn't do anything to Bobcat and William at the moment (whether they had intended to cause her trouble or not) but these assholes seemed like a pleasant diversion.

"Kiss my sweet ass, you gringo pieces of shit!" she yelled and hurriedly crossed the street, making sure to look like she was trying to get away from the guys. She smiled when she heard the muttering and exclamations behind her and their quick footsteps in her direction. She didn't hide her accent, which only made them angrier.

Sometimes being a Queen's Ranger with the duties it entailed was a real pleasure.

Schwabenland, Antarctica

Dr. Abesemmins shivered despite his long johns and coat. Flying on a conventional airplane down to Antarctica was a price he was willing to endure if it got him a chance to speak with Maria Orsitsch.

It had taken him more than a week and a half to think how to persuade both Eva and Patrick that they needed to take this chance to learn more from the Thule group, since they had resurfaced again. The Thule group had been mostly silent, and now the chance to see if they knew more than they had divulged so far was a golden opportunity.

A golden opportunity they needed to take advantage of.

Abesemmins had been shocked when both Eva and Patrick accepted his argument the first time. He wasn't going to look a gift horse in the mouth, though, so he hurried to pack his bags before they changed their minds.

Abesemmins looked out the window as the plane turned to start their landing. There were four of those damned TQB one-person patrol planes stationed in the air that he could see. One country had made the mistake of believing TQB wouldn't fire on unexpected guests, and they had learned they were right.

But the Thule group had no compunctions about shooting down the craft. Seven people on that plane had died and the message coming out of Schwabenland was, "When we say 'no' we *mean* 'no.'"

Message received.

Recently invitations had gone out to a few countries, offering to speak with their representatives to see if Schwabenland would like to form an alliance with them.

This, of course, had caused an uproar in the UN. That circus was getting worse and worse. Even Patrick had to admit Schwabenland allying with another country was probably going to cause a major problem in the UN.

Not his problem.

The plane hit the ice and they experienced only a little swaying as the pilot got it under control. Abesemmins could feel the landing was going to be safe and he let out his breath.

The tension he had felt in the pit of his stomach let up just a little.

Abesemmins was one of twelve delegates from the United States. No one on the plane knew him, so all on the plane figured he had been secluded in some government program or another and they were right—to a point.

He was here to see if he could find the information that those he worked for were seeking.

New York City, New York, USA

Tabitha's alley ended in a small enclave where three buildings came together, giving her about a twenty by thirty-foot area to play. The back doors had rusted metal bars over them, and there was one old light that was trying its damnedest to shine through the grime covering it.

She turned around and waited for them as the five guys entered the alley.

Instead of running right at her, they slowed down and took their sweet damn time approaching.

How typical. Slow down and enhance the terror for the woman so they could feed on it.

There was a dumpster on her right, next to a door that smelled of Chinese food. She eyed the men and walked toward the dumpster, and with the screech of metal on concrete she pulled the dumpster away from the wall. This would ensure the lid, as she flipped it up, would stay open.

She walked back toward the center and lifted an eyebrow. A couple of the young toughs looked sideways at their friends, but no one wanted to admit the little display of strength had startled them.

"Gentlemen," Tabitha started as they fanned out where the alley opened into the courtyard, "and by 'gentlemen' I mean 'assholes'—"

"Now, that isn't the proper way to respect the men around you," the middle tough interrupted and spat on the ground. He was wearing a denim jacket with a black sweatshirt underneath, and his accent sounded maybe first or second generation American to her.

Tabitha, hand on hip, nodded toward his clothes. "What isn't proper is that outfit! Didn't your mother teach you how to dress?" Her face made obvious what she thought of his looks.

A couple of the guys with him started grumbling and the guy in the center put his hands out, pushing down as if he were calming those with him. "Now, that isn't a way to get out of this situation safely," the head dickwad replied. "Neither is talking about my mother."

"I didn't talk about her, I asked her son if she taught you how to dress. If she did and this is what you're dressing in, then you either ignored her or you are as dumb as a rock. No one," Tabitha acted like she was looking down at him, "wears a white t-shirt with a black sweatshirt and an old denim jacket. Shit, didn't those things go out of style last century?"

"Not where it matters, muffin," he replied, raising an eyebrow at her.

"You got nothing to make a muffin rise, asshat. Jean jackets are appropriate in the South, and maybe still with metalheads. You're here in New York in the fucking winter cold. I doubt one girl gives you a second look." Tabitha looked at the walls on both sides.

"You are about to give me a second and third look with a little... What are you doing?" He looked up the walls on both sides too before looking back at her and smiling. "Oh, now you get it? You figure out you have nowhere to run?"

Tabitha turned around and glanced at the two windows behind her, confirming that no one was at either. The guys could hear her just fine as she turned back to them. "I'm just making sure we don't have any witnesses, Ace." She looked at him. "The ass-kicking I'm going to give you five will only give me a few hours' satisfaction, but it's the best I have on offer at the moment so, what's it going to be? Are you all mouth and no action?" She punctuated her comment with a pelvic thrust. "Hmm?"

"Johnnie," the guy on her left whispered, "c'mon, this isn't right."

"Don't be a pushover, Sebastian," Johnnie retorted. "She's as much as dared us to kick her ass. Trust me," he took a couple of steps forward and made smooching noises at Tabitha, "when I get done with her ass, she won't be able to sit down for a week."

As he finished his statement he popped his pelvis toward Tabitha to the catcalls of the guys behind him as they started following him forward.

Sebastian sighed heavily. His cousin was impetuous and fool-hardy. His momma always said one day he was going to get Sebastian in trouble.

He prayed it wasn't this evening. As he followed the other four, he noticed something that concerned him.

Had her eyes just flashed red?

CHAPTER TWO

Schwabenland Base, Antarctica

Maria Orsitsch nodded to her two guards, and both Hans and Horst returned her nod as she stepped between them to enter the meeting room. Their base, once they had brought the heaters online, was a very comfortable seventy-four degrees. All her people were older, but in great shape.

Unfortunately she didn't have the technology to make her people reverse-age as the young queen did.

Horst grinned. "Dress again, Maria?"

She stopped in front of him. "If I knew that a punch would hurt you, I would hit you. A slap against that granite you have for a head would only hurt my hand, Horst." He smiled at her as she continued speaking, "You know I'm not fond of the pants women wear today. Dresses are for ladies, thank you very much."

"Yes," Horst replied as she stepped between the two men to go into the room, "but the pants allow us to see a woman's weapons so much easier than a dress, Maria." The men smiled as they closed the door behind her.

Men! Maria thought. *Freeze them and thaw them out and they still only think of sex, sex, sex.*

Maria set her yellow notepad and pencils down. She preferred to write her notes and her personal shorthand was completely unique, so no one would be able to decipher it.

Except perhaps the Kurtherian. She had asked Bethany Anne twice now to speak with TOM, and the most she had been allowed was communication through one of their phone devices.

"Maria?" Hans called sometime later. The knock on the door took her attention away from the notes she had made during the meeting with the Germans the day before. The history of her country was dramatic, to say the least. Broken apart after the war and brought back together in October 1990, there was a lot of good and bad about the reformed country. It wasn't the Germany she remembered.

Truthfully, none of the countries were anything like she remembered or cared about. Her last meeting was with the United States of America and then she would have to deliver her decision to her people—those who chose to continue following her.

Wherever that led.

"Yes?" she replied, looking up from her notes.

"I have Barnabas out here, from Bethany Anne. He is asking permission to speak with you for a moment."

"That's fine, please let him in." She put down her pencil and stood up.

Barnabas walked in and nodded to Maria, who nodded back. Barnabas was a very peaceful person, at least to Maria.

"*Wie Gehts?*" he asked as the door closed behind him.

"*Gut, und Dir?*" she replied as she took a seat. Barnabas never tried to shake her hand or hug her in any way; he was always formal in their meetings. Of all those who followed Bethany Anne, she found him the most comfortable.

"I'm very well, thank you," he finished in English and pulled out one of the chairs. "Are you ready for this last meeting?"

"As ready as I can be. It seems, to me at least, that speaking with aliens is a more straightforward exercise than talking with anyone from the future—or at least my future—in this world."

"Have you made contact, then?" he asked but then put up a hand, a small smile on his lips. "My apologies. My curiosity knows no bounds, as Frank Kurns would attest."

"Yes, another whose curiosity knows no bounds. You two should be brothers," she replied.

Barnabas nodded. "It was strange, our first meeting. When he and I first got to know one another I had information he wanted, and he was a spring of information I needed."

"Really?" She looked down at her pad and realized it was the wrong one for her notes about Frank, and looked back up at Barnabas. "I thought I remembered him saying you didn't ask as many questions as he?"

He winked. "If we must talk about Frank behind his back," Barnabas started, "then the truth is no one can ask as many questions as that man. Nor," he nodded to Maria's notepads, "does he ever fail to make all sorts of notes in his books about the answers."

Her eyebrows drew together in concentration. "I don't remember him writing much."

"Mmmm." Barnabas put his hands on the table. "Then I would suggest that he was recording the meeting to jot down notes later so he could get more questions in," Barnabas could see Maria weighing that answer, "or he was so captivated with the answers he dared not slow down, and he wrote his notes later."

"More likely the former than the latter," Maria replied. "He did place his tablet on the table when we spoke."

"Mystery most likely solved. I doubt he would trust his memory, as good as it is, without a backup."

"Is it true he is from my time?" she asked.

"Frank? Yes. He was in the Second World War, and has been through a medical procedure to reduce his age."

"That is fascinating. I wish my contact had provided that

information. I can't say I enjoy sitting with Bethany Anne, considering how attractive she is." She reached up to grab her hair, which was getting longer but not nearly as long as she'd had it in the stasis chamber.

"Bethany Anne was attractive before she was healed. You were both attractive in your youth and still are, I believe. However, that is not why I am here to speak with you."

"Yes, I know, Barnabas." Maria picked up a pencil and tapped it on the table. "But you are the only one I feel I can share some of my thoughts with. You just tell it like it is, and don't try to control the situation or my decision."

Barnabas raised an eyebrow. "You don't suspect that I am a vicious plant by my Queen to influence your decision?"

Maria laughed. "No! God, no. If Bethany Anne wanted me to do something I imagine she would have Captain Kael-ven tell me. I'm a sucker for an alien, and she's the only one who seems to have plenty of aliens hanging around her."

"Yes, she does acquire aliens without trying. It is a singularly unique trait," Barnabas replied dryly.

She asked, "So if you're not here to influence me, Barnabas, to what do I owe the honor of your presence?" She smiled, wishing she were fifty years younger. She would have had a chance to turn his head in a complete circle if she'd still had her youthful looks. There had been a reason the *Vrilerinnen* were called 'the beautiful young ladies of the *Vril Gesellschaft*.'"

"I'm here to ask your permission to sit out of the way and watch the people." He smiled. "I promise I will be a ghost. No one will even notice me."

"There are inquisitive people among the Americans who are coming, Barnabas. I doubt they will ignore you." He just shrugged, smiling enigmatically.

Maria wasn't without her own resources. She knew he was different, and old. Ancient probably, although she could never get anyone to admit just how old he was. She had considered it a

It was time for Ambassador Zhou to use the carefully culti-vated alliances and debts China had amassed over the years.

"They did not take everyone," Ambassador Jamil Franklin responded. Ambassador Zhou did love a well-scripted debate.

"Yes, and why is that?" Ambassador Emeka asked. "Is that because they have the ability to know who has our secrets? Perhaps they only look for those who can bring a little bit extra, so to speak, to their hidden goals? I know they claim they are going out to the stars to fight other aliens, but why are they building a giant space station?"

"A *what?*" Ambassador Billony asked, her eyebrows going up in surprise.

"Their space station," Ambassador Zhou took command of the conversation once again. "TQB has been secretly building a space station out in the Asteroid Belt these past three years. We have images from some of our space assets."

"What do they need with a space station?" she pressed, turning from Ambassador Emeka to Ambassador Zhou.

"That is a good question," Zhou replied. "The unofficial offi-cial explanation we hear from backdoor conversations is they are using it for the hundreds of thousands of people they have stolen from our respective countries. The," he nodded to Ambassador Emeka, "cream of the crop they have taken from our countries, perhaps stifling our ability to get ahead?"

Ambassador Billony's lips pressed together. She was new to the group; her country in Europe had recently gone through elections and the old guard had been tossed out. The new presi-dent and cabinet were certainly more bellicose in their speeches against TQB.

It had cost China considerable effort to support the new pres-ident during the elections without getting caught. The race had still been close within a month of the vote, but then an unnamed source or sources had dropped a significant amount of email and other documents that had changed the election. With so much content to wade through, no one questioned who could have shot the two short video clips that showed the president with questionable people which swayed the remaining holdouts and pushed the victory from close to a landslide.

"So how do we stop them?" she asked. "They abide by the rules not to land in our countries, but our people go to other countries."

"They just used that rule to filter out those who weren't serious," Emeka retorted. "The US, so far, allows them to take people from their country. They purchased land and use it for a space terminal. The US hasn't shut them down."

"The decision to change that might be close, I understand," Zhou interrupted, and all heads turned to him. "The present president is not as big a fan as the previous one was. Right now the most that has been done against TQB is to require them to fill out flight plans, which allows the US to test their radar and other defensive locations and target acquisition."

"A lot of good that does us," Billony grumbled.

Zhou shrugged. "It isn't like our people couldn't leave and go to the US anyway, so they would have to admit they are stopping their whole 'land of the free' nonsense if they do otherwise. I know they are stinging from some significant losses of military, science, and advanced technology people themselves."

"Now they know how it feels," Billony replied, "to have your people go to another country and stay there, not coming back to help your own country do better with their new skills."

Many around the table nodded sympathetically. The US was now receiving the rewards for having done the same to all of them and many other countries around the world for the last hundred years. No one here was going to shed a tear for the Americans, who lost some of their own people to TQB.

Mind you, none wanted to admit they might have a country or a government people didn't want to come back to or support, either.

people again, trust me when I tell you that Bethany Anne and her Bitches have a rough way of teaching."

Peter opened his grip, and Sadhi dropped to the ground. "Now, you two grab your tablets and open the book on important people. I want you to write up your story on what just happened and maybe a few ideas on how to make damn sure you can tell when the Queen comes knocking, got me?" he growled.

"Well," Ken offered, "the scary-as-shit red eyes are a unique characteristic."

Peter laughed. "You should be happy. Usually she isn't in such a good mood when those fuckers show up."

"That was a *good* mood, sir?" Sadhi asked. His hand trembled a bit as he pulled up the documents Peter had told him to review.

"Fuck, *yeah,* that was good." Peter turned to depart, calling over his shoulder as he walked away. "Your ass would be *dead* otherwise."

His answer hung in the air long after he had turned the corner, his steps receding down the hall.

Schwabenland, Antarctica

Dr. Abesemmins' credentials passed along with those with him. He looked around at the large cave mouth, which had been cleared and was hosting different types of vehicles. Some had been built recently to go outside the cave, while some looked as if they had been around since World War II. Some of unique design, made a long time ago. Abesemmins wished he could take a look, but his job was clear.

Get in, take notes, ask questions, go back to his job in Washington, DC.

The Schwabenlanders all looked older. Fit, but definitely older. Hell, if his people waited long enough they would be able to come back after they all died, which would certainly be within the next couple of decades, and just take what they wanted.

Or, considering how strong one of the guards looked, perhaps they were not so frail.

Half the group was ushered into a tiny waiting room, and the door clanged shut behind them. Abesemmins looked at the guy behind the glass.

"State your business," His German accent was heavy. J.J. Aspens spoke up.

"US delegation to meet with Ms. Orsitsch."

"I understand you have twelve with you, Dr. Aspens?"

"Yes," J.J. responded. "We have another six waiting outside."

"Makeup of the people outside?"

"Two ladies, four gentlemen."

"Understood, Dr. Aspen. Welcome to Schwabenland." The door on the other side of the small room unlocked as a buzzer went off.

Abesemmins walked out with the rest, and a minute later the others came out of the chamber.

"Doctors?" A middle-aged woman spoke from Abesemmins' right. He turned, and she continued, "If you would all follow me?"

They started after her as she called in a pleasant voice, "Please don't leave the group. That would be very dangerous."

Abesemmins nodded. They had been told of the potential havoc awaiting those who went sightseeing in the base without permission.

The results were often deadly.

Abesemmins guessed there weren't too many lawyers in Schwabenland. If they'd had any to begin with, their curiosity had been fatal.

It took them about five minutes to walk to the conference room through hallways that had nothing interesting to see. Abesemmins, usually good with underground locations, suspected they were close to the entrance and their starting point. However, they must have planned the trip to skip certain areas.

"Remember now, boss?"

"Yes!" she huffed. "Those two snakes set me up!" She puffed a stray strand of hair out of her face.

Jean pointed at the largest Gauntlet. "Is the Proc-101 there going to get scrapped?"

Bethany Anne shook her head. "No, don't misunderstand me. I'm good with," she pointed to the hologram, "those. As for the boys, I'll be ready for them next time. It looks like our favorite saint will be involved, too."

Jean nodded sagely. For the last three years, Saint Payback-is-a-Bitch had become almost a religion unto itself among Bethany Anne's people.

Captain Kael-ven clopped on his four legs down the hallway and nodded to the two Wechselbalg guards who stopped humans from entering the Yollin space on the *ArchAngel* without permission. Occasionally new recruits rotating onto the *ArchAngel* would come down to the Yollin quarters to see if they could spy the somewhat reclusive Yollins.

Last month, a couple of self-professed geeks had damn near had a heart attack when they had been stopped by the guard, only to find Captain Kael-ven behind them when they turned around to go back.

Both had just stood there looking up at him, stupefied.

"Do you mind?" he asked them. "I need to get by to go to my room." He stretched out his arm to point down the hallway.

The two geeks had shaken their heads silently.

"You have to move first," he patiently explained to the two humans. Finally the two Wechselbalg guards picked the two humans up and moved them next to the wall so the Yollin captain could continue on his way peacefully.

This time there were no sightseers.

The door to Kael-ven's suite opened and shut as he walked through. He had figured out that ArchAngel was capable of telling the Yollins apart and didn't mind opening his door for him. He felt like a member of the First Caste every time he walked into his room.

"Captain Kael-ven, you have a call from TOM," the speaker announced after his door closed behind him.

"Answer, please," he replied and walked to his sitting couch.

TOM's voice came through the speaker, "Hello, Kael-ven. I'm sorry to be short with you, but I need to run a bunch of alien races past you."

CHAPTER FOUR

Bethany Anne, Ashur, John, Darryl, and Jean Dukes appeared in the specially built Queen's transference room. It was a thirty-foot diameter, fourteen-foot-high room with simple rubber flooring and two sets of doors. One set went into her private chambers and the other led into the guarded hallway.

The rubber floor was there to help soften the fall if someone had too much momentum when appearing, and it was easy to clean should blood be a problem.

Ashur skidded to a halt at the outside door and barked.

"Welcome home, Ashur." Meredith, the Operations EI for the base station spoke through the speakers. Ashur bolted out as soon as the EI opened the doors.

"Don't be getting into a fight with Bellatrix!" Bethany Anne called. "And kiss the puppies for me!" The four of them heard him chuff in response, and John and Jean snickered.

"It's a lot easier," Jean began as the four of them headed toward the conference room through the same set of doors, "to believe you aren't crazy now that I can understand his communication."

"I don't know," Bethany Anne replied as the doors slid shut behind them. "I kind of enjoyed it when no one but me knew he could communicate. You guys should have seen the looks on your faces."

"Oh. Uh, I always thought we hid it well," Jean told her.

Bethany Anne laughed.

"You do realize that besides reading minds, even if she isn't trying, she gets a feeling for what you're thinking?" Darryl asked Jean.

"Nooo," Jean drew the answer out, "but that might be a little embarrassing to learn now!" She shot a dark look at her man, who shrugged as they continued down the hall.

"Don't worry about it," Bethany Anne told Jean. "We don't advertise the fact because it would only freak people out. I try to push it down, since it feels like I'm a Peeping Bethany Anne. Sometimes, though, like when Ashur was talking to me, it was fun." She looked at Jean. "You need to get your fun where you can sometimes."

Bethany Anne smiled when Jean's cheeks colored. "Not like that, you nympho." Jean's cheeks colored more deeply as the two guys laughed louder than the sound of Jean's punch on John's shoulder.

Five minutes later they entered the special legation room. This one was inside the base, as opposed to the one connected to the docks that was used for security reasons.

Bethany Anne nodded to Omar Kolan, previously in charge of Hotel Operations for the Asteroid Belt, and now elevated to help run the human operations side of the base station. Dr. April Keelson from Medical and Dr. Michelle S. Brown-Williams, who was in charge of food, were at the side of the table with Mr. Kolan.

She greeted the tag-team of Kevin McCoullagh and Yamauchi Stephanie. Lance had pulled them up from the Colorado Base, and they had helped oversee the beginning of the excavation and the building of the *Meredith Reynolds*. They were on her right with Marcus, Bobcat, and William. The smelting area in the belt had finally been disassembled, and the massive amount of raw materials from excavation were stored wherever the hell they could find room. The miners, accustomed to the difficulties of mining in space, appreciated mining out the inside of the asteroid with the new Yollin drilling machines.

It had been a tough but good three years.

"First up," Bethany Anne asked, "the artificial sun?"

Marcus grimaced. He preferred not to call anything artificial, but he had been ruled against with finality when Bethany Anne had asked him his preferred name.

His official choice had been a long group of scientific words that had made one want to use them for a drinking game.

Screw up saying the name, take a drink. People would get plastered in minutes.

He answered, "We've tested all three levels, and they're working. We also tested what might happen in seven different catastrophic scenarios including," he looked at his two friends, "if an idiot got drunk and ran a small Pod into the main Etheric energy collector and overcharged the system."

Bobcat shrugged. "Always assume alcohol will take your worst catastrophe and magnify it."

"Preach it, Brother Bobcat," William agreed.

"And?" Bethany Anne interrupted.

Marcus turned back to Bethany Anne. "It degraded effectively in all instances and we did *not* have any unfortunate accidents."

"What, pray tell, was the likelihood of an unfortunate accident, and what would it have been again?"

"Ah." Marcus scratched his cheek and looked at the table.

"Less than dying in an airplane crash, and instant annihilation for everyone inside the asteroid."

"So," Bethany Anne confirmed, "the only survivors would have been those outside in the dock area?"

"Yes," Marcus admitted.

"Then always assume alcohol is available and sprinkle it everywhere like pixie dust when you conceive of problems with the system. My whole attempt to save that backstabbing blue ball back there would immediately cease being terribly effective if our damn base was vaporized."

She paused a moment, then added, "By us."

Bethany Anne looked at Marcus, tapping her nails on the table to get him to look up at her. "We've had these discussions before, Marcus. I understand you work in probabilities and the chances of a mistake after you, ADAM, ArchAngel, Meredith, the Defense EI, and TOM all go through the design might be vanishingly small, but we can't make a mistake if we can help it."

Marcus nodded his understanding.

"Okay, so when do you want to turn on the main system?"

Marcus' eyebrows rose. "Ah, what?"

Bethany Anne smiled. "I believe you've tested the Arti-Sun effectively, so when do you want to fire it up?"

Schwabenland Base, Antarctica

The American delegation had been speaking with Maria for well over an hour now and Barnabas only had one thing nagging at him.

He couldn't read Dr. Abesemmins.

His mind was a blank. He was a cipher, a problem, a puzzle.

Barnabas enjoyed a puzzle, because it promised new knowledge at the end when you finished putting it together. That he couldn't read Abesemmins' mind was curious and extremely rare, but it was just a hint something could be wrong, not proof —so far.

The Americans had pretty much promised Schwabenland their own small part of the country, similar to the way they had finally provided American Indians with their own land. Unfortunately for the Americans Maria had read up on them, and the American Indians' life hadn't gone too well until they figured out that gambling was the ultimate equalizer. Now, reservations all across the country were pulling in the white man's money legally.

Hell, the white man was driving for hours to drop his money in the American Indian coffers.

If the Indian games management and government handled it properly the Indian people were going to do well for a long while. Perhaps generations to come, if they didn't succumb to greed like almost every other human in existence.

Maria nodded toward Dr. Abesemmins, who had held up his hand. "I apologize, Ms. Orsitsch, but I have a couple rather unique questions, if I may?"

"Certainly, Dr. Abesemmins."

"We understand you have spoken with aliens living in Alpha Centauri. I am not questioning that in any way whatsoever, but we are curious if you have perhaps had contact with another group of aliens...the Grays?"

All faces turned to Maria. "No," she replied. "I'm aware of the aliens called 'Grays' and do not believe I've spoken with any of them." She smiled benevolently toward Dr. Abesemmins, who had been nothing but incredibly respectful when he had asked questions so far.

"Thank you. The second question is, have you ever heard of aliens called 'Kurtherians?'"

"*SNEEZE!*" Barnabas ordered in Maria's mind, and she immediately held up a hand, turned her head away from those at the table and sneezed loudly.

"Please do not recognize the name Kurtherians, Maria," Barnabas suggested, leaving the final decision in Maria's lap.

Either way, this man was now Suspect Number One on his list of leads.

Maria fanned her face, closing her eyes and turning her head back away from the table again. This time she turned in Barnabas' direction, and her eyes widened when she saw him sitting in the chair.

Then they narrowed as she looked at him before she sneezed once more and turned back toward the table.

She smiled at the table. "I'm terribly sorry. I'm usually not very allergic, but perhaps something came in with your clothes. I do apologize again." She turned toward Abesemmins. "I'm sorry, Doctor. You asked about an alien species? Kurthurans?"

"No, madam, 'Kurtherians,'" he corrected.

"No, I have not. Are they important?" she asked. "I've heard of maybe a dozen different species, but Kurtherians," she paused to make sure she was pronouncing the name correctly, "are not one of them."

"I understand. They are," he told those who had written the name down in their notes, "a rumored race and a passion of mine. My apologies for taking a gamble and asking during this limited availability of your time."

At least three heads nodded in understanding, all researchers Barnabas knew, having read their surface thoughts.

They continued talking for another twenty minutes when there was a knock on the door. Hans and Horst opened it and walked in. Soon the Americans had been herded out of the room, with Maria following to see them to the exit. She turned and whispered into the room before she closed the door behind her, "We will talk later, Barnabas."

Private residence outside Chicago, IL, USA

The former president sighed as he hung up the phone. He leaned back in his chair and used his foot to move it so that he was looking out the large window into the beautiful winter landscape at the back of his house.

He was going to get pulled back into this mess one last time.

He had left two envelopes for the new president three years before. The first was the traditional letter from the outgoing president to the incoming one. That was expected, and it had held similar thoughts and recommendations to those the president before him had left at the start of his own term of office.

The second one was simply labeled, "Ignore at Your Peril."

For the first year after he left office the relationship between TQB and the USA had been cordial, and he had hoped the decent working relationship he had built with Bethany Anne would continue with the new president.

It had not.

From the first they hadn't gotten along. Both had large responsibilities, but only one of them had real ability to back it up.

The USA had a large capacity to be tactical, and some damned impressive weaponry and people. Bethany Anne, on the other hand, could drop a rock in the middle of Colorado. That she *wouldn't* was an assumption the wags in the government had finally decided was the gospel truth.

If you could do something but you wouldn't, where was the threat?

He continued looking out the window, knowing he was going to pick up his personal phone and make that call. He owed the world another try. Hell, he owed his family another try.

He breathed deeply and reached back with his left hand, moving it a couple of times left and right before he grabbed the cell phone and pulled it back around.

He grinned just a little as he used the digital assistant. "SIRI, call Wonder Woman."

. . .

QBBS *Meredith Reynolds*

The all-system warning lights and alarms screamed, and all non-essential personnel were told to get inside.

It might have been nice to have everyone see this new technology turn on, but Bethany Anne wasn't willing to gamble on a small mistake vaporizing her people.

Watching it happen on video was going to have to be good enough.

Those working to bring up the new artificial sun were working inside the main engineering rooms. One with the controls, another for the machinery with glass between them. "When you close the loop between the two systems from the Etheric side, come back here and hit the button to complete the links," Marcus told Bethany Anne. He licked his lips as he watched the two screens showing the Etheric energy pull for the systems.

He touched the commands and the lights in the middle of the massive cavern dimmed, leaving everything in the inky blackness that the absence of light always produced.

The smaller Etheric taps were being rerouted to the Arti-Sun.

"See you guys in a second." Bethany Anne stepped into the room with the Etheric tap machinery and closed the glass door behind her. One second they could all see her, the next she took a step and was gone.

Marcus watched the readings and reached up to wipe his forehead. Then there was a slight uptick in Etheric energy coming into the system. "Four, three, two...one!" Marcus called and slammed his hand onto the desktop when the energy input spiked a thousand-fold and the slight humming from the room next to them became a roar.

"YES!" Marcus screamed triumphantly. "We have connectivity

and the capacitor is not being slammed! The Arti-Sun is acquiring energy per stated calculations. Meredith?"

"Yes?" the EI responded.

"Are you seeing anything outside normal parameters?"

"No, Marcus. I am running the agreed testing parameters, pulling the energy through the Etheric iris using different diameters. So far it is running... One moment."

Marcus' mouth opened. "One moment?" he asked as he turned to review the systems.

Bobcat and William stepped up. They had worked to stay in the background on this project.

"What the hell?" William asked, and started using the far-left monitor as well as checking additional screens.

Bobcat worked with Marcus. "That doesn't look right." He pointed at a chart on Marcus' screen.

"Tell me something *new*, Bobcat." Marcus snapped as he worked to see what Meredith was doing.

"Uhhh...new. Okay, here's one. I think I found a girl?" Bobcat told his friend.

"That's nice, what does it taste like?" Marcus asked as he touched areas on his screen to show two additional input charts simultaneously.

Bobcat snorted. "Jackass! I said girl, not another beer."

"You have no other love but beer, Bobcat," Marcus answered.

"Folks?" William interrupted them.

"Yeah?" Bobcat answered, and leaned over to look at where William was pointing on his screen.

"Oh, fuck us again," Bobcat blew out. "Marky Mark, take a look over here."

Marcus looked quickly over to William's screen and then returned to his for a second before he turned back to William's and leaned in. "What the hell?"

"It's Morse code," William answered. "Bethany Anne is testing our system."

"How the..." Marcus shrugged. "Meredith, translate the Morse code and use it to figure out the next fluctuation. Adjust appropriately."

"Done," Meredith replied moments later.

Thirty seconds later when Bethany Anne appeared in the glassed-in room the hum of the machines behind her receded to a solid midlevel bass, one you could feel in your chest.

She opened the glass door and the sound increased, and then closed it, blocking most of the noise from reaching them once more.

"How was that final exam, guys?" she asked as her phone went off in John's hand. He took the call.

"Fine, boss. Did you have to scare us so bad?" Bobcat asked.

"How did you handle it?" she asked.

"Swimmingly, I assure you," Marcus answered. She went up and patted him on the shoulder. "I'm sure you did, but how confident are you that the system will work if we get unexpected Etheric fluctuations?"

"UEFs?" Marcus looked at her, confused. "TOM never said there were any UEFs, and before you say anything, I did ask."

"I love TOM to death, which might be foreshadowing if he keeps talking to me in my head at the moment, but I've asked him if he is an Etheric know-it-all and he admitted he wasn't. Who's to say there isn't a normal hundred-solar-year Etheric flash?"

"We passed, right, boss?" William interrupted and gently kicked the back of Marcus' ankle.

"Yes, you passed," she agreed.

"Bethany Anne?" John called.

She turned and raised an eyebrow. He wiggled her phone. "Call from the president." She made a disgusted face and he explained, "Sorry, *ex-President*, not the PITA."

"Oh, then okay. Toss it here." John flipped the phone to her, and she snagged it out of the air and put it up to her ear. "Hey, ready to leave Illinois?" she asked with a smile.

The voice laughed on the other side of the line. "PITA?"

"Yeah, our not-so-hidden acronym for you-know-who," Bethany Anne replied. "One second." She turned around to see the rest of the team in Arti-Sun engineering high-fiving each other and passing around small glasses of alcohol.

Good thing EIs didn't drink.

ADAM, confirm Meredith is running Arti-Sun for the next few hours.

>>**She is in full control now. Marcus set that up previously. It requires an override from him, with your permission in advance, to change that.**<<

At least he was thinking ahead. She noticed Dr. Brown-Williams had sidled up to Marcus and seemed to be initiating a conversation. Marcus was oblivious that his little sun stunt had attracted the food scientist in maybe a romantic way.

Who knew?

She turned back to her phone. "Okay, I'm back. What do you want me to do, and who put you up to this?" she asked the ex-President.

"That obvious, or am I bugged here?" he asked.

She tapped her lips. "No, not bugged, but if I lied about that it would be funny as hell to hear about your security detail scrambling all over your house trying to find how we knew."

His frown came through clearly through the call. "No, I don't think so. My wife would not appreciate having our walls ripped apart and destroyed as they tried to find your technology. They would evict us under eminent domain or some shit, and we'd never see the inside of our house again."

"Oh, yeah. Guess that might suck for a joke after all."

"Well, the request is that you come to an event in Europe, along with a select few power players in government and business, to try and bury the... Poor choice of words. To see if we can negotiate any sort of agreement for the technology when there aren't a bunch of cameras and egos involved. Well, egos on parade, anyway."

"So, no lights, cameras, or recordings?" she asked.

"Can't promise anything, but I was told it was supposed to be a pleasant meeting of walking around and chatting. No one is going to say anything, admit anything, use anything in the meeting as political ammunition, etc., etc. Believe as much of that as you want."

"And you?"

"For my sin of being able to call you and have you take my call, I've been asked to attend with you."

Bethany Anne snorted. "You done gone and fucked up, haven't you?"

"Apparently."

"What's the wife think about this?" she asked.

"She's coming around to flipping everyone the hell off and kicking their arrogant asses to the curb. Thinking about how she spoke up for them for the past three years is starting to grate on her nerves."

"Told you so." Bethany Anne smirked.

"Wow, and I thought queens were above that."

"Not this one. I've decided being regal is passé." She turned around to see Marcus waving his hands in the air as he explained what he was thinking.

"And boring," he added.

"*Especially* boring. How those kings and queens in the past did it, I've no idea," she agreed as she turned back to his conversation.

"So, will you do it?" He got back to the reason for the call.

She shrugged. "I don't expect it to accomplish anything, but I'll give the dead horse one more chance before we put it six feet under."

"Have your people call my people?" he asked.

"How about we have Gabrielle call you back?"

"Yeah, that works, too," he agreed before asking, "She's still with Eric, right?"

"One second." Bethany Anne barely covered the mic on her phone and yelled to Eric, "Hey, potato head!" She waited for Eric to turn toward her. "You and Gabrielle are still tight, right?"

"Who's asking?" Eric replied, confusion on his face.

She held up the phone, her other hand still covering the microphone. "The president we like."

Eric grinned. "Oh, then tell his wife that yes, Gabrielle is still very taken."

Bethany Anne put the phone back to her ear. "Did your wife hear that?"

"Yes, she's nodding that she did. She came into the room a few seconds ago to let me know dinner was ready."

"Okay, so Gabrielle will call you and it will get set up. You guys go eat. Catch up with you later."

They said their final goodbyes and hung up.

CHAPTER FIVE

<u>Schwabenland Base, Antarctica</u>

Maria Orsitsch didn't know whether she should be fuming or allow her curiosity to overcome her anger at Barnabas for exhibiting powers he hadn't divulged before.

Or both.

She had expected the man to disappear after whatever he had come here to do was done, and was surprised to find he was still at the table and sipping coffee from a mug someone must have brought him when she came back to the meeting room.

She told Horst to stay out and entered the room, closing the door behind her. "That was an interesting display of talent I hadn't expected you to perform, Barnabas."

He dipped his head in acknowledgment and continued sipping his coffee.

She pulled out her chair and sat down, placing her elbows on the table. "Are there additional surprises I might expect?"

He put the coffee on the table. "Why would I tell you this, Maria?"

She stabbed the table with a finger. "I was under the impression your queen was one of the legations working to acquire our allegiance? How about we start with that?"

"Then I think you have mistaken something, Maria." Barnabas picked the mug up again and took another sip. "What you have at this base is impressive, and your skills and weapons are commendable, yes." He put his coffee cup down a second time and wrapped it with both hands. "But if you want to be frank and talk like two adults, nothing here," he nodded his head toward the door, "is of value to the Etheric Empire."

"Then why all this aid?" Maria asked, annoyed. "Your people have helped us keep Schwabenland a free country. For what purpose are you doing this? Further," annoyance crept into her voice, "you ordered me to sneeze!" She sat back and pointed a finger at him. "You could be manipulating me right now."

Barnabas raised an eyebrow but said nothing.

"Well, answer the question!" she demanded.

"Maria, there was no question. You are irritated because you feel out of control. The fact you felt *in* control was due to a misperception on your part. You and your people are protected as a courtesy, and to keep you safe from a fight you can't win."

"A fight with whom?" Maria waved her arm toward the door. "Those unknown flying saucers? Their technology is better than some of ours, but not enough to allow an easy win over us. I doubt they can make it too far into this fortress."

"Not them, although we suspect they would be worse than you think. No, with Bethany Anne."

"Why would *she* be a problem?" Maria asked, now totally confused. "She's never been belligerent to us, nor have we done anything to TQB."

"Let's play a game called 'Suppositions,' Maria." Barnabas offered. "Let's pretend that the following happened: Schwabenland, for whatever reason, was overcome by a foreign power. Any of the majors—China, for instance." Maria's sudden grimace was all Barnabas needed to know she could see the results of that path. "Or America, with their present President and attitude of World First?"

"Bethany Anne is responsible for that," Maria fired back, "not us."

"No, Bethany Anne is responsible for saying 'No.' Nothing else, and she's stuck to her guns on the subject. Apparently her consistent position on this has infuriated those who believe that since they have combined into larger and larger groups of adult children who throw nation-sized temper tantrums, she should change her mind."

Maria sat quietly for a moment before commenting, "This was our path, you're telling me?" He nodded. "So, without her taking the heat and flying overwatch up there to make sure no large country came after us, we would presently be speaking United Nations-ish?"

Barnabas smiled. "Yes, that was the scenario we saw happening. Those who run psychoanalysis on Bethany Anne decided that someone trying to take over Schwabenland by force would push Bethany Anne to act. If they had, she would retaliate, but with small groups, like the airplane you shot down. You were on your own."

This time Maria thought for a few minutes on his words.

She looked into his eyes, her blue irises beautiful in the artificial light. "You don't want us?"

Barnabas shrugged. "I've not had personal discussions with the Queen on the subject. As far as I can guess she would be happy if you joined, or okay if you stayed. She suspects that if someone in the world possesses your technology and doesn't share, it will be the final match that lights the gunpowder of World War III."

"And where will she be?"

"Across the line in the stars, Maria." Barnabas' voice softened. "We haven't hidden any of that from you."

"You are leaving this mess as it is?"

"Maria." Barnabas paused, then sighed. "Maria, we are less than five hundred thousand souls out there, and we are going to fight a race that is the boogeyman of the entire Milky Way. I don't think you need to add 'Parent the Earth' to our list of things to accomplish."

"If you don't, who will?" she replied, her voice resigned.

"How about Earth itself?" Barnabas asked. "It isn't outside the realm of possibility they will figure this out themselves. Bethany Anne's taken on the responsibility of making sure Earth has the option to stay free, but what they do with that freedom is up to them. If we take the option away then *we* are the subjugating empire, and it will be brother against brother and sister against sister at that point. Is this what you are asking us to do?"

Maria looked down at her lap, her fingers fidgeting. "That's what it will be for us, except in our case it will be us against our grandchildren and their children's children." She looked up at Barnabas. "Most of my people aren't thinking this way, but I know it." She patted her heart before she looked to her left, as if she could penetrate through the solid mountain and see Germany itself. "We do not have the strength to deny a world that would beg us for help."

She sighed, resignation and sadness closing in. "We are a people out of time, Barnabas, in a world where those who live in it have no idea what world war was really like, and frankly," she turned back to Barnabas, "don't know they are at the beginning of one again."

She shook her head. "No, I was pulled into a war and forced to help a group of people I had no desire to support. Schwabenland was the negotiated price for our help. I will not go through that again."

She looked at Barnabas. "This is what I would ask of your queen, Barnabas."

. . .

New York City, New York, USA

Tabitha came out of her room in the suite she and the Tontos were staying in while in New York. There was a knock at the door. She raised an eyebrow when Hirotoshi walked over and opened it and spoke with Katsu outside for a second.

Closing the door, he turned to Tabitha. "Kemosabe, why is the New York Police Department coming up here?"

Tabitha acted innocent and shook her head. "No idea. Anyone we know?"

"Yes, it is Inspector Clouseau." Hirotoshi's heavily accented answer made a mashup of the detective's name.

She pointed at him. "You know that isn't how his name is pronounced." She walked past Hirotoshi, who eyed her like a father watching his teenage daughter who had gotten away with something and he wasn't quite sure what yet.

There was a knock at the door, and Tabitha practiced her smile before opening it and greeting the man on the other side.

"Why, Detective Cleusah, what a surprise seeing you again!"

"Is it?" he asked her. Detective Cleusah was five feet ten inches, dark-haired and probably fifteen pounds past his prime weight, but he still had the muscle from his twenties. "I happen to be—"

"Hold that thought one second," Tabitha told the detective and shut the door on the rest of his sentence. She turned around to find Hirotoshi ten feet behind her, his arms crossed over his chest. "I'll just take this outside."

She turned back to the door and stepped out, causing the detective to rapidly back out of her way. Katsu smirked when Tabitha looked at him. She rolled her eyes, grabbed the detective by his suit jacket, and started toward the elevator.

"Where are we going?" he asked the headstrong woman.

"Ix-nay on the alking-tay, 'k?" she muttered as they walked to the elevator. It dinged and she practically grabbed the detective and pulled him in as her finger stabbed the Door Shut button over and over again.

It finally closed for her.

"Tabitha, what the hell is wrong with you?" he asked, exasperated. Since meeting her two years before when a lot of justice came calling in New York—by a woman vigilante no less—Detective Theodore 'Ted' Cleusah had both looked forward to seeing Tabitha and dreaded it at the same time.

He could never pin the situations over the last two years on her, but it seemed like every time she came to town, unexplained stuff happened to less than savory individuals. The one time he had been able to absolutely pin her to a location, she'd had many eyewitnesses that it was a clear case of self-defense.

"I can't just want a moment of your time, Ted?" she asked him in a breathy voice.

"No!" He put up a hand. "Been there... Well, sort of, and no thanks. Sorry, but the concept is a lady on the street, a freak in bed. Not a freak on the street and God-knows-what in bed."

Tabitha chewed on her lip. "Damn, I hadn't considered that a problem. I thought 'freak in bed' forgave all sins."

"I have plenty of freak in my normal existence. I don't need more at home," Ted answered as the elevator reached the lobby.

The doors opened and Tabitha looked to her right and winked at Ryu, who had lobby guard duty at the moment. This was going to piss him off, because he wouldn't be able to follow her this evening.

"Why can't we stay in this warm hotel?" Ted asked as she dragged him by the hand into the chilly night outside.

"Because the hotel has a lot of ears." She took a left. She let go of his hand and put hers in her pockets. "Okay, since you aren't here to ask me on a date, what can I help you with?"

Ted grimaced. With her accent Tabitha could make just about anything indecipherable to a normal English-speaking person.

discussion like this?" he asked. He refused to read Maria's mind for a reason he still didn't quite understand. It did make it more interesting to work with her, but the frustration level was considerably higher.

"Because as a man of justice, you are one of the few I trust implicitly to do this for me." She leaned back in her chair.

Barnabas looked at the woman, considering her request. "I don't have a reason to be involved, Maria."

"No, not one that is part of your Ranger group, that is true. However, would you do it as a friend? For me, Barnabas?" she asked, her eyes wide enough to draw Barnabas into reading her topmost thoughts.

He closed his eyes and nodded. "Yes, I will make the request." He opened his eyes again. "But the decision is Bethany Anne's." His eyes pierced her soul. The absolute and granite assurance that she couldn't press him another inch was in them.

Why, she wondered to herself, *weren't you in Germany a hundred years ago?*

the report had described and her comment about the guys just blowing off steam.

"Probably about two-point-five or three."

"What do you call these guys besides 'Bitches?'" Ted asked.

"Me?" Tabitha asked, and Ted nodded. "I call them friends."

"What *are* you people?" Ted asked, not really expecting an answer.

"We are the Earth's best chance of staying free. We are Bethany Anne's people, come hell or high water. We are her law and her Justice, all wrapped up in a no-nonsense group of humans who will walk through hell and clean it the fuck up. Satan had best hope Bethany Anne never points us that way."

"Is that what you were doing here in New York?"

"In a way, yes. I've been chasing some assholes for a while, and I'm back."

"Those guys tonight just got in your way?"

"More like they accosted Justice and she kicked their asses. If they had truly been in my way I would have taken them out, or if not me then Barnabas, a Bitch, or Bethany Anne. And actually, God help them if I ever call *her*."

"Why?"

"Because it means vengeance is coming, and she doesn't drop flowers behind her. She's a great leader, don't get me wrong, but she has a 'zero bullshit' policy and that's what I deal with...bullshit. There is a lot of bullshit in our lives, and I'm pretty good at rolling with it. Bethany Anne?"

"Yeah?"

"You probably wouldn't have found those dicks."

"She would have killed them?" Ted asked, his eyebrows drawing together. "For being rude?"

"Ummm... Accosting a woman is not simply rude, it's a horrible experience. This time the little woman fought back. But no, Bethany Anne can do things far worse than killing them and before you ask, I won't tell you. Hell, I don't know them all."

"Then why do you follow her?" Ted asked.

Tabitha took a sip of her coffee before answering. "Because she saved my life, and then she saved my soul. I get the chance to pay it forward, so I'm going to do it. The man I call my father might be back one day and I'm going to be there, right beside Bethany Anne, to welcome him back."

"Your father?"

"You wouldn't know him. His name is Michael. Once we have our present task completed, I know we'll be searching and we *will* find his ass, I guarantee it."

"He's dead, gone, lost, or what?" Ted asked.

"He's definitely lost. Bethany Anne says he isn't dead, but I don't know why she says that. They have a connection, that's all I know, and I trust her completely. If she says he's alive, then he's alive. She tells me to clean up New York City, I come here and start cleaning up New York City."

Tabitha cocked an ear and touched her tablet to drop the sound field. "There's a mugging going on. Leave it alone or fix it?"

"Ah, fuck!" Ted exclaimed, and Tabitha smiled. She was up and out of the diner before he stood.

There was a twenty-dollar bill on the table, and Ted had never seen her put it there.

Who the hell was this woman, really? Or should he be wondering "what?"

He started jogging to catch up.

He heard a whistle to his left as he exited the diner and started running that way. He came up to an alley and could hear Tabitha's voice.

"Look, shithead, I don't care if you need the money to put your momma through college, stealing it from this woman isn't the right answer. Getting a job, perhaps after taking a bath, would be a good start."

Ted grabbed for his badge but hesitated, then slid it back into his pocket.

This was what he had been researching, wasn't it? Now he wasn't so sure he should have made up the lie about having a girlfriend.

He walked as quietly as possible in the shadows, to see Tabitha between a woman crying on the ground and two punks.

The larger, taller white guy spoke to her. "Look bitch, we takin' this money, and whatever fucking money you have too." He pulled out a ten-inch knife, the glint off the blade in the poor light flicking up and down the alley.

"That's not a knife!" Tabitha replied in an Australian accent. She reached inside her jacket and the guy jumped toward her screaming, "Aaiii!"

The man shot across the alley and there was a loud *crack*, then a crunch as his body hit the wall and slumped down. Simultaneously, Tabitha's foot came back down.

"Well, that was fucking rude," Tabitha huffed, and spoke to the second guy. "You giving me back her purse and money, or are you going to take a dirt nap like your friend over there?"

"He... He dead?" the second punk asked, looking at the guy crumpled on the ground.

Tabitha spared a glance at him. "No, not yet. His lung is bleeding from where my kick broke his ribs and punctured it. I can hear the blood causing problems already." She turned back to him. "I suggest next time not stabbing first and asking questions later."

The guy handed the purse to Tabitha, who helped the lady to stand up. "Check if anything is missing."

"Will you help Jim?" the second thug asked. "He might not be much, but he's the only friend I got."

Tabitha looked at the punk. "You got a name?" He nodded. "So tell it to me already!"

"Thomas."

"Okay, Thomas. I'll help your friend, but if he ever pulls this shit again I'll let him die, understand?" He nodded to her. "Just so you know, that guy behind me is a cop. Don't be getting ideas."

Ted walked up behind them and watched as Tabitha pulled something out of her jacket. It was a syringe and a vial. She pulled some of the liquid into the syringe, then knelt and ripped his shirt. "If you want to help, Ted, call him a paramedic. This will save his life, but he's still going to be sore as shit and need some bandages and help. I'm not making him feel all better, and sure as hell I'm not kissing his boo-boos." She stuck the needle between two ribs and administered the shot.

Ted pulled out his phone and started typing on it. "What are you giving him? Is it a medicine that's going to get you in trouble?"

"Not likely. Nothing will show up in his toxicology reports."

"More secret stuff?" Ted asked.

Tabitha stood up and turned around, putting the syringe with cap back on and vial back inside her jacket. "Ted, I've been shot, stabbed and fallen from three-story buildings... Well, actually I jumped, but that's neither here nor there. I need this product to help me survive in my job. That I helped this loser is a weakness of mine, not a strength. What he got was what was coming to him. I really helped Thomas, who just wanted a friend in life. I was there when I was younger. Maybe together, the two of them will find the help they need."

Tabitha started walking away. "Wait!" Ted called, his eyes switching between Tabitha and the two punks. He was trying to decide what, if anything, he could do to keep Tabitha with him.

"Got to go, Ted. Enjoy the view while you can." She patted her ass. "Sirens are coming this way, so you'll have friends soon." She turned around and walked backward, looking at him. "Don't bother with the hotel, we've already checked out." She blew him a kiss and then turned back around and walked around the corner, disappearing in the dimness.

"Shit." He sighed, his shoulders slumping.

QBBS *Meredith Reynolds*

"Bethany Anne?" Meredith asked from the speaker. "Barnabas is calling for you."

Bethany Anne looked at her tablet and the list of e-documents she needed to review. Even though she pushed a lot of it off to ADAM, who could give her the necessary facts for a decision, it was still a lot of work.

She highlighted a third of the documents quickly and sent them to her dad. He had too much time on his hands, she was sure.

"Okay, I'm good. Put him on." She looked up to see Barnabas' face hovering in the air in front of her. "What's going on?" Then she noticed the room he was in. "You in Schwabenland?" He nodded.

"Yes, home of the free-but-frozen," he replied.

She nodded. "Tracking someone down?"

"Yes, I've got a lead on the people who keep attacking us. They might have sent someone here to speak with Maria as part of the American delegation."

"Oh? Do you think the US is involved in this, then?"

"No, I don't believe so. No one on the team knew this person, and I couldn't read him."

"Sorry," she interrupted, "but did you say you couldn't read him?"

"Yes, I did."

"How often does that happen?" she asked.

"Rarely. It's happened before, but the percentages are fairly remote it could happen without this person having help."

"Okay, tell me the rest of the plan, Barnabas."

"I'll jump in my Pod in about thirty minutes and follow them. They've left, but ADAM is tracking the plane for me. If they deviate from the flight plan they gave the military I'll know."

"Let me know if you need anything, and I appreciate the update—"

This time Barnabas interrupted. "My Queen, I have something else." He gazed into the camera and straight into her eyes.

Bethany Anne raised an eyebrow. "Uh oh, for you to be so formal this must be good."

"Maria Orsitsch has requested permission for the Thule group here in Schwabenland to emigrate to the Etheric Empire."

Bethany Anne shrugged. "Okay, that was the decision we expected out of all of their options. Why is there a speed bump?"

"She wants to provide some technology transfer to the Germans before they come with us."

Bethany Anne thought about it a moment. "What technology? We haven't told them before they couldn't share technology, so how come she's asking about it now, and why is she worried enough to ask *you* about it?"

"She wants to hand over the core concept of their version of gravitic drives. Those versions are extremely power hungry and can't send ships out like ours, but it's an advancement that could cause problems in the world."

Bethany Anne tapped her finger on her lips. "Yes. ADAM did some analysis with Frank and Jeffrey on this. I'll have Frank call Maria and explain the potential ramifications. Let's see what she decides to do after that." He started to interrupt, but Bethany Anne put up a hand. "I'm not saying their permission to emigrate is denied if they choose to deliver the technology. I'm stating that they need to know, and the absence of a 'yes' should at least cause her to think long and hard about it."

He nodded his understanding.

"Okay, follow up with me on your tracking. Those assholes have been a major thorn a bunch of times, and if we can find out more about them I'm game."

"And if we find out they're deep in the USA?"

"Barnabas, what do you do to cancer if it's in your best friend?"

"Cut it out," he replied.

"Yes, we will cut it out, with or without permission."

Barnabas' eyebrows went up and Bethany Anne smiled. "The answer, before you ask, is that it's easier to ask for forgiveness. Maybe. Depends on what they're doing. According to Mason Jayden, his people were working on the technologies that could handle those flying saucers, but he never found out where the technology originated. According to Maria the advancements we've seen were not from her, and according to TOM, some of the spacecraft's abilities we've seen are well known to half a dozen alien races and so could be from any of them. I'm not a huge believer in allowing a cancer like that to exist while we're off fighting in a different solar system."

"Understood, Bethany Anne."

They said their goodbyes and Bethany Anne looked back down at her tablet after he disappeared. She still had over sixty-two documents to discuss with ADAM and decide which direction to take.

"Fuck me," she muttered as she called up the first.

asked, his face going slack for a moment, then snapping back to alert. "Well?"

"Well, what?" Tanya asked, "I'm not sure I got your question the first time."

"What will you have, ma'am?" Barry asked, interrupting the conversation.

She reached over to grab David's drink and smelled it. "Is this Glenlivet?" Barry nodded. She smiled. "I'll have one the same way, thank you." Barry went to get the lady her drink and she turned back to David. "I'm sorry, what was the question again?"

David pursed his mouth and shrugged. "Beats me."

Barry returned and slid Tanya's drink to her. She reached inside her clutch and pulled out three twenties. "This should cover anything for myself and David, yes?" Barry nodded and accepted the bills, then went back toward his conversation at the other end of the bar.

"Wow, thank you." David picked up his glass. "I'm sorry you got stood up, but I can't help but think this has been a wonderful night for me so far."

"Well, just think of it as me paying in advance," she told him, taking a sip from her drink.

"For what?" David asked, daring to raise his eyebrows, flirting for the first time in a long time.

"Shall we say, 'services to be rendered?'" Tanya replied and raised one eyebrow, holding up her drink in a toast.

"Damn, that works for me," he agreed, and clinked her glass.

The next morning when David woke up, he tried to remember the previous night. He looked around his room; the sheets and the bed were definitely more messed up than usual, but he didn't see anything out of the ordinary that a night of drinking too much might not have caused.

His head wasn't pounding, so thank God for small favors. He got out of bed and walked past his dresser. His gun and everything he normally would drop on the dresser was there, nothing missing.

He continued into the bathroom and stopped.

His bathroom had been done in white. White marble countertop, white wood siding, and white tile set at a forty-five-degree angle with gray grout.

He took a couple steps and reached down. The red panties were easy to see against the white. He picked up the folded piece of paper. Apparently the dream had been real.

Hello David,

Thank you for a fantastic dinner, and even more wonderful night. I hope another girl gets as lucky as I did when they get stood up.

Because Up should be your middle name.

David smirked and continued reading.

I hope my payment in advance was sufficient, and I look forward to your payback.

All my best,

Tanya

He turned the note over a couple of times. She hadn't left a phone number, so how were they supposed to get together for payback?

QBBS *Meredith Reynolds*

Darryl and Scott milled around the crowd standing in the large cavern. In the future this cavern was probably going to be used for shipbuilding, refurbishment, or disassembly, but for now it was a good place to host thousands of people who had emigrated to the Etheric Empire.

This was a smaller group—maybe three thousand. Although it had been over a year since the last jihadist had tried to join and assassinate Bethany Anne, the two guys mingled with the audience to see if they could get a read on anything bad before it happened.

Presently there was a ten-foot-tall stage on one side of the room. It was kept clear for these events when Bethany Anne, John, and Eric would arrive.

Bethany Anne had delivered thirty-two of these speeches so far and she understood each might be the final speech for the new people joining them, so she always gave her best effort. Each month more impediments for people to emigrate were put on people on Earth.

In the end, those who were joining ran the risk of giving up their lives, and they needed her best effort to help them decide which way they wanted to jump—with her, or back to Earth.

Scott nodded and smiled at a young family. The dad seemed hesitant to interrupt him; perhaps he was an introvert. Scott looked around to confirm nothing seemed amiss and stepped closer to them.

"How are you?" he asked the parents as he fist-bumped the young dark-haired boy who smiled at him.

"Excited!" The mom smiled and her green eyes lit up. "This is it, right?"

"Depends," Scott answered, playing with the boy's hair. Scott looked back at the parents. "If you mean, is this the meeting where you join us, then yes, this is it. You have the option to say no, and we'll take you back to Earth fairly soon. Or you can say yes, and you renounce all your ties to Earth's countries and join the Etheric Empire."

"Why do we have to renounce our ties?" the dad asked.

Scott looked at him and shrugged. "That was more an Earth condition than ours. However, if you are from Australia you don't. There are seven other countries that also don't care. For us, those of us in the Etheric Empire, we tend to think 'Humanity first,' so we don't mind if our countries get their panties in a twist. The world is a big place and countries are your people, your kind. It's natural for a human to join and want... No, *need*, to be a part of a group. Well," Scott waved his hand toward the crowd, "this is that family now. We are tied together by a desire to move ahead, and to protect the world whether they all deserve it or not." He put his hand down. "Further, we're going to make our own way out there. We aren't sure we'll ever see the Earth again, so this base station or another planet might be your home. We don't know. But," Scott nodded at the podium, "the Queen is about to appear, so catch me later if you have questions, okay?"

The man agreed as his wife gushed with excitement, and the boy tugged on his dad's shirt to be held so he could see better. The dad agreed, and Scott grabbed the little guy and easily lifted him to sit on his dad's shoulder. He continued his walk through the crowd.

The cavern was lit by the same portable Arti-Sun technology used in the large cavern, smaller and with small gravitic support, which allowed Meredith to move them around as she needed since this cavern wasn't in use all the time. The units were about six feet wide and ten feet long, and there were translucent panels in place to diffuse the brightness. Eyes had been damaged by looking directly at them—the effect was no different than looking at the sun from Earth.

"Your attention, please," the speakers attached to the walls boomed. "This is EI Meredith. Please direct your attention to the stage and reduce your talking." There was a pause. "That means you too, Mr. Killsbury."

There was laughter from Scott's left. Meredith always found one or two boisterous people in the group and called them out by name. It was a small reminder that she could hear and see just about everything on the base. With operations being her responsibility, she considered the emigration acceptance event to be a high priority.

The light above dimmed a little, and the light on the stage increased. There was a five- to seven-second wait before John,

Eric, Bethany Anne, and Ashur appeared, and the crowd went wild as Bethany Anne smiled and waved.

It was always something unique when people appeared out of nowhere.

Ashur chuffed and then pranced around the stage. "Oh hush," Bethany Anne told him as she waved to the crowd on both sides of the stage. "You love this and you know it. The lights make your white coat practically shine."

Ashur barked at a child in the audience and wagged his tail before turning toward the three humans and chuffing again.

"Not my fault," John insisted. "Bellatrix doesn't like the limelight. She's happy to stay with the puppies and visit the kids at the Academy."

It had been a little over two years since TOM and Bethany Anne finally figured out how Ashur was sending messages to her and how she was picking them up. A ten-minute modification in the Pod-doc now allowed most of those around Ashur to understand him directly as well. There were a handful of devices that could be handed out to help Ashur communicate with those who did not have the modifications.

Bethany Anne finally stopped waving and turned her palms face down, using hand gestures to quiet the group.

Okay ADAM, pipe me through the speakers.

>> **Understood.**<<

"Welcome to the QBBS *Meredith Reynolds*, humanity's first base station and the home of the Etheric Empire." Bethany Anne's voice could be easily heard throughout the crowd as she walked back and forth on the stage.

"Let's cut to the chase on one of the most confusing terms here, which is 'Empire,'" she started. "As you know, my title right now is 'Queen Bethany Anne,' not Empress. That's because we here are a group of people who understand that our sense of identity is a shared purpose to protect those back on Earth. We aren't ethnically similar; we have members from all over the world. We don't all share the same language, although everyone has been fitted with translation tools and an implant. Eventually, I'm told, we will all speak the same tongue. Our culture, such as it is, will grow with us as we engage in the mutually satisfying effort of making damn sure our families, friends, and loved ones back on Earth get to do whatever it is they want to."

Bethany Anne stopped in the middle of the stage and looked over the crowd. "Remember that. We are going out there," her left arm pointed up and to her left, "to give those on Earth," her right arm pointed down and to the right, "options. It is not and *cannot* be our responsibility to make sure they do the right thing on Earth."

Her voice was a little somber. "Think about that. We might save the Earth from aliens only to have Earth destroy itself." Her voice brightened. "Or they might figure out their problems and when we or our children or children's children come back, Earth might be Utopia."

Bethany Anne spread her arms to encompass the crowd. "The only reason they have the opportunity to become Utopia is because of you. Your willingness to take chances. Your belief in fighting, or supporting those that fight, and the courage to challenge an unknown future."

She pivoted and started walking down the stage to her left. "Now, I know that some of you—in fact, many of you—are also fed up with what is going on with our world." She turned and started back the other way. "And frankly, many in the world are upset that you chose to come up here, so don't expect any accolades from Earth as we go through the gate." She haphazardly pointed behind her. "It's that way, if you're curious."

A bunch of heads turned to stare at the far wall, perhaps to

CHAPTER EIGHT

New York City, NY, USA

While the Tontos checked out the house, Tabitha walked around the large mansion and wondered what it must have been like when Michael lived there.

She knew he had underground rooms. Bethany Anne had chosen to not visit there, and frankly, no one was sure if it was possible to get into them or if it was even safe.

A large metal door had been installed to cover the access. Bethany Anne had told them she wanted it solid but not airtight, so if Michael should ever need to get past the door there was a way in.

Tabitha walked down the stairs that led to the suite of rooms or whatever Michael had built for himself under the house and sat down on the last two steps. She stared at the metal door for an hour, wondering what her father had in there. Wondering what he was like before he met Bethany Anne, before he had started to soften some from being around so many women in his life, and she grinned.

Michael was challenged for sure by both her and Bethany Anne. She had figured out his temperament and fought back so much he had secretly asked to have her replaced, but Bethany Anne had stopped that. Tabitha had almost wet her panties from laughing when she found out that Bethany Anne had told Michael the only replacement available was a gay man. End result, Michael had retained her, and for that alone Tabitha would be forever grateful.

Michael had given her a man she could believe in. A man who, she knew from the bottom of her heart, would have supported her for the rest of what would become a very long life. He had taught her to believe in herself because that was the only way she could do what he demanded.

And when she produced miracles, he made her feel good about what she accomplished. He told her many times that the cleanup of the mess in South America would not have been as successful without her.

She smiled. Michael never blew any smoke. If he said you did well, then you absolutely had done well. Not just by the measure of today, but by the measure of people who had worked with him over centuries.

It was a hell of a team to be a part of, and she felt proud that she was. The most recent member of Michael's technical team, perhaps, but for sure not the last.

Bethany Anne had promised they would get him back.

"You know," Hirotoshi spoke softly from the top of the stairs behind Tabitha, "we always have a bolt hole. There is likely another way in."

Tabitha shrugged. This time she had heard him at the top. "Probably? I have no idea if anyone but Michael would be able to use it, though, and it seems a little voyeuristic to me to look inside his bedroom."

Tabitha turned to look up the stairs and put up her fingers an inch apart. "Even if part of me desperately wants to have something personal of his, you know?"

Hirotoshi came down the stairs and stopped, dropping down to sit a couple steps above her. "Yes, I understand, Tabitha."

"We going to find them, Honcho Tonto?" she asked.

"Them who?" he replied.

"The bastards who have blocked me so many times already."

"Yes, we are close. Who knows, maybe tracking them to New York was right and they are within only a few miles of us right now."

Tabitha laughed. "Damn, you know how to turn me on, HT." She made wringing motions with her hands. "Just let me have a few minutes with each of their necks, you know?"

"Get in line behind the Queen."

"Yeah." Her shoulders fell. "Like I'd have a lot left over after she was done."

"It isn't your station to replace her Justice, should she choose to implement it."

"I know, but she does this 'Kick them into the Etheric and they disappear' shit. I want them penalized."

"How so?"

Tabitha thought about that a few moments. "Give me a minute…or ten. I'll come up with something suitable, I'm sure."

"Well," Hirotoshi stood up, "you might wait until you find out who they are before you select a punishment." He started back up the stairs, his feet barely making a whisper. "I'll check on the group, Kemosabe."

Tabitha stood up and followed him, working on her foot placement to minimize the sound. "I'm with you and learning, Number One."

"It was hidden," Katsu related as he, Tabitha, and Hirotoshi looked at the laptop sitting on the large wooden desk. "False bottom in one of the drawers." He pointed to the lower left drawer.

"Well, scoot your butt over and let Momma give this a try." Katsu stood up and Tabitha slipped into the chair. It was an old IBM Touchpad. Katsu had already plugged the power supply in, so she hit the power button. The old floppy disk drive made its chucking noise as it checked for a boot disc, then the fan started to spin.

"Damn, these old IBMs last forever," she murmured as they waited for the memory count. The first screen came up.

"Windows *WHAT?*" Tabitha choked out. "Wow, who the fuck was old enough to use this antique OS?"

"Michael," Hirotoshi suggested.

Tabitha looked down at the chair, then around the small library-looking office they were in and considered where he would have come up from his rooms, and breathed out. "Holy shit." She rubbed her hands on the leather armrests and looked up at Hirotoshi. "I'm sitting where Michael would sit?"

Hirotoshi nodded. "Most likely."

She pointed to the laptop. "This is coming with me."

The final boot screen and password request came up, and she held out her hand. "Katsu?" He placed a USB device in it, and she looked on both sides of the laptop to find the USB input. She pulled out her tablet and set it on the table, and went through her own security to bring it up. "Achronyx?"

"I'm here and listening, Tabitha," the tablet replied.

Tabitha looked up at both men, a question on her face as she spoke so softly even the vampires could barely hear her. "Who changed his programming to be nice?" she asked and they both shrugged.

"Do you want something, or are you just wasting my time?" the tablet asked.

"Oh, neverfuckingmind." Her voice was normal again.

"Glad to have the normal Achronyx back," she told the tablet. "I've got a small task for you. Old IBM laptop running Windows software, and I need you to hack in past the password. Be careful. The OS is old, but the guy who was running the security at that time was top-notch."

"I'm always careful," Achronyx replied.

"My ass you are," she retorted. "Remember Budapest?"

"That was a miscalculation about the ability of the original owner of the server," the EI answered.

"Whatever floats your digital boat. You've been warned," she told it.

Tabitha leaned back in the large leather chair and turned her head this way and that, and realized she could still smell the tiniest amount of Michael on the leather. "This chair needs to go back with us." She looked up at Hirotoshi. "It'll be a present."

He nodded his understanding.

"Security is bypassed," Achronyx interrupted at the same time the OS continued past the login screen to finish boot-up.

"Lord of the fantastically crappy GUI," she muttered as she looked around at the large old icons. "No wonder those old dudes can't see shit." Then she whistled and pointed to the screen. "This has a 'Bethany Anne' folder on it."

"I think the Queen needs to be made aware of this," Hirotoshi suggested.

"I... Just... But..." She slumped. "Okay."

She leaned back in her chair and sought the connection she had with Bethany Anne.

Bethany Anne?

Yes?

Busy?

One second. Nope, good now. Tabitha, what's up?

I'm at Michael's house.

Okay.

We found something.

Ooooookay.

I'm pretty sure that we have Michael's old laptop, and it has a folder about you on it.

What's it say?

I haven't opened it, she replied. *Who do you take me for?*

A hacker that doesn't know when to stop looking. Is Hirotoshi or Ryu behind you?

Yes, she admitted. *Hirotoshi.*

That explains the failure of Tabitha to be Tabitha. So he suggested I know there's something about me, right?

Got it in one.

Do you need to go into that file, other than for the itchy fingers all hackers have to find out shit they shouldn't know about? Bethany Anne asked, amusement coloring her question.

Dammit, you make it sound like a disease! Tabitha replied.

It is a mental disease to be sure, but we all have mental conditions and yours works for you. It's why you make a good Ranger.

Tabitha didn't know how to respond to that statement. She hadn't considered her insatiable curiosity an asset to her Ranger role.

No, I don't.

Then stay on target. From what I remember, Carl and probably Michael had some hellacious backdoors all over the—

YES! Tabitha's mind link practically screamed back.

Ouch, Tabitha! Bethany Anne exclaimed. **What the hell?**

Tabitha leaned forward, her hand moving the little red nub on the keyboard to maneuver the cursor around the screen.

I bet those assholes don't know all the backdoors Carl had!

You think there are some Frank or ADAM can't find?

Those guys are fucking geniuses, but Michael and his hackers had decades to set shit up. There could be databases that don't hit the web itself.

Not that you probably waited, but permission granted to review.

Zhu's eyebrows raised. "That easy?"

Shun took a swallow of his beer. "That much time in the forest gives one time to contemplate what is right for one's country and what is good for one's leaders. They often have not matched."

Jian picked up his bottle and tapped Shun's before he took a swig and put it back down.

"Do we have a target?" Zhu asked.

"Yes, a small manufacturing company about an hour south of Zhengzhou," Shun explained. "Just received the instructions before I left." He turned his wrist over and looked at his watch. "Woo's people are going to leave in about an hour and go down there by truck to capture the employees who are working the late shift."

"An hour?" Jian asked, and Shun nodded.

"I'm not having it." Jian reached into his back pocket and pulled his wallet out. "I'm driving, guys." He dropped another fifty on the table and stood up, no imbalance in his steps. Shun and Zhu watched their friend for a second as he walked toward the door.

"It's prison," Zhu muttered.

"Or execution," Shun added.

"For Bai!" Zhu exclaimed. He slid out of the booth past where Jian had sat and started after their friend.

Shun grabbed his hat and slipped back out of the seat as he put his hat on and agreed, "One more time, for Bai." He followed his friends.

Whatever Shun's ancestors wanted, he might not be able to give them. He would, however, protect his countrymen from the enemy.

The problem was, this time the enemy was the government.

New York City, New York, USA

"Are you telling me," Tabitha spoke into her tablet as she looked at the laptop screen, "we finally got the slimy bastards?"

"Yes," Achronyx and ADAM answered her at the same time.

She hated it when Achronyx ignored ADAM. For an EI, Achronyx could be a turkey sometimes. She was surprised ADAM didn't digitally slap Achronyx.

She, Hirotoshi, Ryu, and Katsu were in Michael's office. The treasure trove of backdoors Michael's laptop accessed allowed them to finally follow the money trails her team's work had uncovered.

It all made sense.

The assholes were in Boston. Not New York as she had thought, but they were close enough.

She'd had Katsu buy a new laptop when he had gone out shopping earlier, and she had virtualized Michael's laptop OS. In the event something went wrong, they wouldn't lose the vast amount of access it provided. With the new laptop, she could work at speeds that would have caused Michael's laptop to seize.

She slid back in her chair. "ADAM, are you sure?" She chewed the inside of her lip.

"Yes, Tabitha. The financial records show the money trail all the way through the four locations you searched previously."

"Sonofabitch," she whispered. "Location of these guys?"

"Achronyx has the Boston address, and I can confirm, using satellite imagery in place, that the site is guarded."

"That makes me feel better, not worse," Tabitha replied. "Since when do those that sleep well at night need guards? ADAM, please notify Barnabas I need to speak to him."

"Done."

"Okay, let's drop, ADAM. I'll speak to you later."

"Understood," ADAM confirmed and terminated the call.

Seconds later Barnabas called. When Tabitha accepted the call, he got down to business. "I understand you've had a breakthrough?"

"Yes. We got the bastards, Barnabas, but there are guards and other issues. I'm considering doing this a little differently than normal."

"What, no three-story falls?" he asked.

"I'm doing better with those. Just last week I fell four stories successfully."

"Number Two, that would be funny if I weren't sitting here wondering if that story is true or not."

"I'll leave you wondering," Tabitha replied.

"Yes, you do that while I hear your plan," he agreed.

"Okay, so here it is..." she started, and proceeded to lay out her idea.

South of Zhengzhou, Henan Province, China

Jian pulled the car around the back of the manufacturing plant. The three men had changed out of their uniforms, and hoped the people inside would listen to them. If not, well, they had their weapons in the car, and perhaps they could frighten them out of the plant.

Shun had put his captain's hat inside a bag, which he grabbed as Jian shut off the car and they got out. It was a little past two o'clock in the morning and they were wearing sweaters to deal with the cold.

Shun walked up to the back door and knocked. When no one answered, he knocked louder.

A muffled voice came from inside, but it was unintelligible.

"Open up," Shun called. "You people need to get lost!" He spoke to the person behind the door, trying to keep his voice down but loud enough to pass through the door and be heard.

The door opened a crack, and someone inside asked him to repeat what he said.

"The government has cut orders to take you hostage against TQB for some reason. You need to clear everyone out of here!"

"Who?"

"The government!" Shun was getting exasperated. Usually if you mentioned the state, it got someone to show their face quickly and their backs as they ran away soon after. He looked back at Zhu, who shrugged. He turned back to the door. "May we come in? We need to get out of sight."

The door opened, and Shun's mouth dropped open.

It wasn't a countryman standing at the door, but a European who was smiling.

And his eyes seemed to glow red.

Hands reached out and grabbed all three men quickly, pulling them into the building. The door shut and the light outside flickered, then burned out, leaving the back door in darkness.

Shun, Zhu, and Jian stood looking at those in front of them.

"I am Stephen from TQB. We appreciate your warning, but as you can see," he swept his hand toward the large manufacturing floor, "there is no one working tonight."

Jian spoke first. "You knew."

Stephen nodded. "Yes, we knew. We have been at odds with governments for years, now. They have been holding people hostage to try to force the Queen's hand, although this is the first time we have no interest in a company and the government is moving against us."

"Why, then?" Zhu asked. "We were told this building was owned by TQB."

"Oh, it's *a* TQB, just not us," Stephen smiled. "Either a paperwork snafu, or perhaps someone hoping the government would shut their competition down."

"Then why are you here?" Shun asked.

"Because my queen doesn't want innocents hurt, and she is particularly perturbed by the Chinese government," Stephen explained. "Those who work here took maybe three to four minutes to clear out."

Shun looked at his watch. "You have maybe fifteen minutes before they get here, probably closer to thirty or forty-five. You can leave."

"What would the fun be in that?" a young American man behind Stephen asked.

Stephen turned toward the young man. "Peter, not everyone enjoys a fight as much as you."

"I'm getting rusty. It's been a little while since our last good fight," Peter answered.

"It's been what, four weeks?" Stephen asked him.

"Five weeks, three days and," he looked at his wrist, "three hours."

Stephen turned back to Shun. "You can see we have some anxious fighters wishing to make sure the brass get the idea that messing with TQB, whether the right or the wrong TQB, is a bad idea."

"But some of you will be killed," Shun admonished.

"No," Jian interrupted looking at the men, "they won't."

Shun and Zhu turned toward their friend. "Why not?"

"These are similar to the ones we chased in the forest," Jian replied.

Stephen smiled. "Ah, I was wondering why you smelled familiar. You are *Baô*, are you not?"

Jian's eyes darted to his friends and he tried to catch Stephen's eyes and shake his head, but it was too late.

Shun asked, "Is it true, Jian? Are you part of the Sacred Clan?"

Jian shook his head, his shoulders dropping. "No." He straightened and looked his two friends in the eyes. "My family and my parents left the clan in the night, scared the Sacred Clan would track them down and take what was most precious to them." Jian pointed a thumb at himself, "Me."

Zhu asked, "Why?"

Jian shrugged, "I'm not sure. My parents were silent about what they knew. I think I was supposed to be a female child for the clan's plans, and the leaders had planned to kill me so my parents could have another child without upsetting the government. My mother found out about my sex early, and they spirited me away in the night."

"They wanted to kill the males?" Shun asked. "That's—"

"Backward, yes," Jian finished. "It had to do with a prophecy. I've pieced together the story over the years."

"You still have the smell, Jian," Stephen interrupted the three friends. "Can you change?" Jian shook his head. "I imagine you might be able to, but you've never been taught and the change is not strong enough to work on its own unless you get highly emotional."

Zhu snorted. "Well, that closes the discussion, then. Jian never gets emotional."

Jian shrugged when everyone looked at him for an answer.

"Let me ask the three of you one more question," Stephen started. When he had their attention, he continued, "Do you want to stay in China, or are you done?"

Jian shrugged, "My parents."

"Can be grabbed safely, if you will tell me their address and go with a team to fetch them quickly." Jian nodded his agreement. Stephen turned to Shun, "You?"

Shun hesitated only a moment before nodding. "I'm done with a government that would take their own people hostage."

"No family?" Stephen asked. Shun shook his head.

Stephen turned to Zhu, "You?"

"I'll go, but my parents will stay. They are in the backcountry, and haven't seen me in three years. I never gave the government my real address or name. I've sent my parents enough money over the years, so my brothers and sisters can deal with caring for them now. But if I could send a last letter?"

Stephen nodded. "Very good then. Peter?"

Peter called over his shoulder, "Karen, Timmons!"

Those in front could hear a female cursing as two people came forward. "Sir?" the woman asked. Apparently she got over her frustration at not being there for the fight before she made it to Peter.

"Help Jian here with his parents. Take Transport Three. When you get there, it will stay with you. The *ArchAngel* just released another transport for us down here. When you finish, take Jian and his family up there."

"Yes, sir."

Stephen spoke again, "All three of you should go. You don't need to be here when the PLA gets here."

"How bad is it going to be?" Shun asked.

"For the PLA?" Stephen asked, and Shun nodded. "Not bad. Well, except for their vehicles." Shun nodded his understanding, then followed Jian and Zhu out the door behind Karen and Thomas. Both of the TQB personnel walked with a hunter's grace.

"People," Peter cracked his knuckles, "get yourself prepared, and *Thomas?*" he yelled.

"Sir?"

"Take care of the lights," Peter finished and smiled, thinking about the fun to come.

CHAPTER TEN

All Guns Blazing, Outer Docks, QBBS *Meredith Reynolds*

The bar was deceptively big.

Bobcat, William, and Marcus had started out with a plan: open the first bar in outer space. Then they decided they wanted the *best* bar in outer space.

Finally they decided they wanted a place where adults could mingle with adults, but the children of their friends could come in as well.

That required some interesting changes to the architecture. The problem was more, 'form follows function.' The guys thought long and hard about what was needed in a bar, and who would probably patronize it.

First, you had solo drinkers looking for a place to enjoy a drink around people, but not necessarily be part of a crowd.

Second, you had different-sized groups of drinkers. Also, there were those who wanted to dance or blow off steam—maybe play darts or hook up.

That all took room.

Then you needed a place that children could join in, which meant a separate area. Not for the children, William argued, but for the adults who wanted to drink without worrying if a child was going to see them and join the next generation of alcoholics. Bobcat thought that was odd, but Marcus agreed with him.

"Look," William told Bobcat. "You'd start drinking in the morning if you could get away with it."

"What do you mean?" Bobcat asked. "I gargle with vodka and cinnamon every morning."

"I'm sorry," Marcus interrupted, "you use what?"

Bobcat turned to his friends, surprised his two buddies didn't know this trick. "Vodka. The recipe is one cup vodka and nine tablespoons of cinnamon. Mix them together in an airtight container and store it for two weeks to let the flavors combine, then gargle." He looked at his two friends. "What? It fixes halitosis."

Marcus' eyes opened wide and he turned to William. "I'm shocked."

William shrugged. "I'm not. The fact that Bobcat knows how to mix his liquor so he can drink in the morning is maybe a little surprising, but it doesn't rise to the 'shocked' level."

"No," Marcus shook his head and pointed at Bobcat, whose head was pivoting back and forth between them, "not that he drinks in the morning, but that he knows the word 'halitosis.'"

William's face split into a huge grin and reached over to fist-bump the scientist, who winked at Bobcat.

Bobcat looked at William and put up his left middle finger. "You're Friend Number One." He put his other hand up with the middle finger extended to Marcus, and looked at him. "And so are you." Bobcat pulled his left hand around and put both hands, middle fingers extended up toward Marcus, "Actually, *you* get to be Friend Number Eleven."

"Yes!" Marcus crowed, hands raised in the air. "I get turned up to eleven!" He turned to William, lowering his arms. "That's the joke, right? Turn something up past ten?"

"Yes, that's right," William agreed to laughter all around. "But it makes my point, Bobcat. You're fine with alcohol twenty-four hours a day. Not everyone thinks that's acceptable."

"Especially around children," Marcus added.

"I blame your inability to have a hangover," William commented. "It makes you less sensitive to the evils of drinking."

"Just because I don't suffer myself doesn't mean I don't suffer in quiet sympathy with you poor schmucks," Bobcat replied. "You should know your limits. My limits happen to be superior to most men's."

"You mean every man's," Marcus corrected. "I've seen Wechselbalg who have trouble keeping up with you."

"Why do you think I gargle every morning?" Bobcat grinned. "Training is the most important part of any good regimen."

William's face went blank, then he looked perplexed before turning to Marcus. "Could that be right?"

Marcus inquired, "What, are you asking the rocket scientist if gargling alcohol would help one's ability to not have hangovers?"

"Uh, yeah?" William replied.

Marcus shrugged. "I have no idea. I'd have to set up research to figure it out."

Bobcat raised his hand. "I'll volunteer!"

Both men turned to Bobcat and barked, "No!"

Now All Guns Blazing had the kitchen in the middle, splitting off the family-friendly bar and grill from the adult bar and recreation area. Both sides of the kitchen had a bar with stools, but one side had tables and booths for eating and the other had high tables, a dance floor, darker booths for private conversations, and an area for darts and other games.

There were a dozen private rooms on two levels that could be rented for either business meetings or parties.

Or both.

The large dock area on the *Meredith Reynolds* was growing. Storage, warehousing, housing, and businesses were built to handle all the externally-focused roles and activities. There were two high-speed magnetic trams that delivered people back and forth between the docks and In-World.

One of the main features of All Guns Blazing was the large viewing deck with a window twenty feet high and sixty long that allowed everyone to see out into space. The deck, reached by stairs from either side, was the premier draw for the bar, and it had taken Team BMW weeks to finally come up with a design that passed the engineering and defense teams' approval process.

It was quieter usually. The view of space caused most to stand or sit and drink in the splendor of the universe.

Except for tonight.

Tonight, All Guns Blazing was hosting a get-together of some old hands celebrating the Anniversary of the Battle in the Everglades.

It was only one of the many times each year the teams got together to pass along the stories from the beginning.

The beginning that had started five unique people down the path to saving the Earth.

South of Zhengzhou, Henan Province, China

Stephen stood in the shadows on the roof of the two-story building enjoying the crisp air. Beside him, Peter kept his hands in his pockets. Both men watched as two PLA transport trucks turned onto the street and headed in their direction.

One of the trucks missed a gear change. The grinding noise was clearly audible before the driver was able to slam the gear home and continue to the parking lot below.

Todd and his Guardian Marines were downstairs, behind the Wechselbalg who were hiding in the shadows of the machines.

"You know," Peter remarked, "I'm getting pretty tired of just humiliating these people."

Stephen looked at the young man. "Desiring more blood, young Wechselbalg?"

Peter's eyes flicked to Stephen. "Not what I meant—at least not that way. I mean I'm tired of keeping the gloves on, Stephen. Every time we do this we keep the carnage to a minimum. It isn't slowing them down."

"This," Stephen pointed at the two trucks pulling into the lot below, "isn't about them. It's about us."

"Oh?" Peter asked curiously. "How so? I get that we're trying to make sure others aren't hurt by attacks on us, but how is this about us rather than them? If we made it hurt more maybe they wouldn't try so damned often."

"Think about the future, Peter. Think about twenty or thirty years from now. You will have *how* much alien blood on your hands? It's going to mess with your mind. I don't think we need to go out there with years of human blood on our hands as well."

The trucks disgorged troops. The two men could hear the shouted commands and then the door, which they had locked, was forced open, and boots flowed into the room below.

"ADAM, drop the null-communications shield," Stephen directed.

"What if they do something that hurts Bethany Anne? What then?" Peter asked as he got undressed, then the two of them walked to the edge of the building.

"Well, then there will be no gloves," Stephen replied as he stepped off the edge and dropped behind the troops below.

The roar of the Pricolici transfixed the men as two monsters fell from the sky into their midst.

Private First-Class Chung was the third man through the door into the dark warehouse, and he turned to the left and aimed his QBZ-95. The man couldn't see anything, but his gut was telling him to run. He swept the area again.

Two of the men had lowered their weapons, and Chung hissed at them. He'd been out in the forest for a short tour, and he still trusted his gut.

"What are you hissing for?" the first asked and rolled his eyes. "There isn't anyone to fight. This isn't the wilds, and you need to stop blaming your time there fighting the cats when you jump at shadows!"

He had barely got out his remark when a primal roar from outside startled everyone. Men twisted around, aiming back at the door as fear rolled in from that direction, forcing them to fight the urge to run farther into the warehouse.

Chung never stopped looking around the building. He saw the wolf, its eyes flashing yellow, streak out from behind the nearby CNC lathe and then leap. The animal's jaws were coming straight for his throat, and he pressed his trigger in reactive fright. Two bullets slammed into the wolf, throwing its trajectory off enough that it collided with him but bit his arm, not his neck.

His gunfire was enough to warn those who had turned around to look back over their shoulders, but few bullets were fired as people dressed in black slammed into them. Guns were ripped out of their hands and growls joined the roars coming from outside.

Chung screamed as the wolf's jaw snapped his arm, and his fingers released the gun to drop beside him as he landed on the floor. He tried to ignore the pain and reached for his knife.

A booted foot stepped on his left wrist, pinning it to the floor. Chung looked up into an American face that said something in English. While he didn't understand the language, the gun barrel in Chung's face needed no translation.

He slowly pulled his hand away from his knife.

"That's a good choice, mate," Todd stated. "I'm sure Tommy over there will heal, but if you stab him with that silver knife you got there I'm pretty sure Stephen won't give a shit if Tommy rips your throat out for real next time."

"You got that right." A male voice, half-human and half-growl, caused Chung to turn his head.

Where there had been a wounded wolf a second ago, a naked human male was getting to his feet. Chung's eyes widened in fright when the man tossed two slugs onto Chung's chest. "I think these belong to you."

Stephen bent his knees and landed gracefully. He had worked on his Etheric skills since TOM and Bethany Anne started playing with Etheric forces and antigravity. He hadn't yet figured out how Michael went to Myst, but he was able to lighten his weight.

John thought his trick was fantastic, and made him watch the opening sequence in Underworld where Selene dropped from a significant height right onto the stone, then stood up and walked away.

Looking sexy the whole time.

His arrival was noticed when hundreds of pounds of snarling Pricolici landed and started tossing around bodies like a kid tosses a present after opening it on Christmas morning and reaching for the next.

Stephen smiled and *pushed* his fear. There was a soldier on his left who was pulling up his QBZ and Stephen was there in a blink, yanking the rifle from his hands before elbowing his helmet. The man went sideways hard enough to take out another who was trying hard to overcome the double dose of Stephen's fear plus having a seven-foot-tall werewolf howling and cursing gutturally so close to him.

Peter, bitching when one man pulled his pistol and shot him, tossed the soldier he was holding. Stephen watched as Peter grabbed the gun and bent it enough to make it useless, then put his large misshapen hand under the shocked soldier's armpit and threw him. The soldier flew fifteen feet, only to stop when he bounced off of the cement wall of the warehouse and landed unmoving in the few pitiful shrubs outside.

There wasn't much light in the parking lot. Two soldiers just pulled triggers, and four others went down under friendly fire.

Stephen, enhancing his speed, reached into his jacket and pulled out a pistol with modified tranquilizer rounds and rapidly started shooting those who seemed the most likely to cause them problems.

Then he shot the rest as Peter howled in frustration. "Oh, be quiet and see who we have left in the trucks, Peter," Stephen ordered.

"Theresss gooeesss myyy fuunnn," the huge Pricolici bitched as he jogged over to the trucks. The drivers' doors were open, but there was no sign of the drivers.

"Cleeannn,' Peter called.

"ADAM, bring them down," Stephen called, and in seconds eight-inch antigrav plates came down and floated by the trucks. "No, Peter!" Stephen yelled at the Pricolici, who was eyeing the soldiers who were running away. Stephen commanded, "Change back, or we'll have another talk."

Peter shook his head in the negative, and moments later he stood in front of the vampire. "Do you," he started to ask before he turned his face to spit something out next to the truck. "Do you always have to threaten to beat the shit out of me again?"

"Yes," Stephen agreed. He grabbed one of the floating plates, then got on his knees to find the right spot under the bed of the transport truck and locked it in place.

Peter started down the other side of the vehicle, putting the plates on as Todd and his people began the process with the other truck.

Stephen grabbed the next plate. "You need to control the Pricolici, not allow it to control you. If you don't, there will come a day when a very tough decision will have to be made, my friend. I'm not going to make it easy for you now and have to do something I'll forever regret in the future."

"Yeah, well," Peter answered, locking his third plate in place, "the last time you kicked my Pricolici ass it got the message pretty well. The hackles on the back of my neck stand up, and then my monster brain remembers you breaking my legs and my left arm and slapping the shit out of me."

Stephen locked his fifth plate in place. "That kind of power needs control or its benefit is lost. It's what killed the berserkers. Individually they were indestructible, but with a good team that practiced, you could take one down easily."

Peter bent down to look under the PLA troop truck. "You knew berserkers?"

"Huh?" Stephen asked and then, recognizing Peter's voice was coming from under the truck, bent to stare at the young man. "Did I know berserkers?"

"Yeah," Peter replied. "I've always admired them. They often helped break up shield walls before they could get set. A useful thing in fights, I was reading."

"Yes, I knew two."

"So tell me about them," Peter asked.

"What do you want to know?" Stephen asked. "They tasted pretty good." He winked at Peter and stood up, moving to the next plate.

"Hey!" Peter called as he grabbed the next floating plate. "You can't say they tasted pretty good and then drop the story." The two men locked the last plate at the back of the truck and walked to the front, where two of Todd's Guardian Marines were affixing the last two plates.

Stephen patted him on the shoulder. "How about you get dressed? Talking with a naked man isn't the biggest deal to me, but you're causing a ruckus." Stephen pointed at some of the female Wechselbalg, who were dropping tied up PLA soldiers outside of the building.

Peter looked up to the roof. "Well, shit."

"Oh, don't be a wimp." Stephen grabbed Peter under the arms.

"What the hell are you... FUUUU—" Peter screamed as Stephen took three fast steps toward the building and threw Peter up. The sound of Peter's landing caused Stephen to smile. The werewolf finished yelling, "UUKKK!"

"Hurry up," Stephen called to him as he turned to find Todd with a smile on his face. "Are the packages ready to go, Todd?" Stephen asked the Guardian Marines' leader.

"Aye, sir, that they are." Todd grinned even wider when Stephen's lips pressed together.

"I'll get my Queen back one day for giving me a title," he complained, and then smiled when he heard Peter's loud 'Sono-fabitch!' when he landed after jumping from the roof.

"ADAM, two presents to return to base."

"Understood, Stephen," ADAM confirmed through the receiver in Stephen's ear. It vibrated the bones and produced sound, so no one else would hear it.

Moments later the two huge PLA transport trucks lifted into the air, accelerating in speed the higher they went before the night swallowed them both.

"You know that rocks hurt like a bitch, Stephen?" Peter came up beside him. "That roof had a shitload of them."

"Then next time, young and unlearned," Stephen looked at Peter, "I suggest you think ahead about your clothing needs."

Military Base, Kaifeng, Henan Province, China

"No, sir," Private First-Class Mi told his commanding officer. "We lost communications with them right after they said they were entering the parking lot, sir. We have not been able to contact them since."

"What could be the problem?" Captain Zhia wondered. "This was supposed to be a secret mission."

"Sir?" Radar Operator Bolin called. "We have two strange craft heading in this direction."

Captain Zhia stepped over to the radar operator and hit a button on the console. "Those are too big to be planes. When was the last time this equipment was looked at?"

"Sir, last quarter per regulations," the radar operator answered. "Look, they're coming this way."

"Should I hit the alarm, sir?" another radar operator asked, seeing the two unidentified objects approaching.

"Where did they come from?" the captain asked.

"We picked them up coming from Zhengzhou, sir, ten kilometers this side of the city."

The captain's eyebrows drew together. "Show me."

The radar operator pointed to the location on the map.

"No, no, no, no, no, no," he murmured, and picked up the phone. "Give me the base commander."

Five minutes later two hundred men, all with weapons at the ready but dressed only in underwear, were standing on the edges of the runway. They watched in confused silence as two large empty PLA troop transport trucks crashed out of the night in the middle of the base's main runway.

The base commander ground his teeth as he waited for the four men detailed to look inside the transports, but seconds later they confirmed no one was in the trucks. The base commander turned around and growled.

"Someone find my damned men," he told his sub-commander as he stalked off toward his office to call Beijing.

All Guns Blazing, Outer Docks, QBBS *Meredith Reynolds*

"So there were the four of us," Eric told the four men and two women at his table. Thirty had been picked to be a part of the evening's festivities. The backdrop was outer space as the guys told stories at different tables on the viewing deck. Each time they held this celebration, they would invite a handful of team newbies, whether Wechselbalg, Marines, Operations, Navy, Engineering, or Defenses.

They shared some drinks, some food, and stories. Together they grew by passing on the emotions, the pain, and the effort to fight through the fear to do what was right.

For each other, and for the world.

Eric pantomimed holding his rifle, looking left and right. "The four of us thought we only had one Nosferatu to deal with. Remember, we were entirely human. No enhancements at that time. Nosferatu were fast fuckers, stronger than Cement-head over there..."

"Heard that, Escobar!" John called over his shoulder, and resumed his own story.

Eric winked at his table. "Stronger than John, I mean. We were out in the Florida Everglades, and if you don't know that part of the United States, it's hot, muggy, and filled with water mingled with small patches of land and alligators. It was getting on toward the evening and we had a fucking Nosferatu to take down and there were four of us. We'd been fighting these sons-abitches for months across the United States. We'd lost a lot of good men, and we had just one vampire to help us. This little switch of a girl with black hair..."

"Heard that, Escobar!" Bethany Anne sang before she went back to her discussion.

"I mean this full-bodied woman with raven hair—"

Bethany Anne called to Eric, "You're so full of shit!"

Eric rolled his eyes and looked at Bethany Anne. "Why can't I tell my story here?"

"Do I need to come over there and beat your ass, Eric?" John asked.

"Okay, he didn't, but he called me a prick so I asked him what Bethany Anne had said about crap-level cussing and he looked over my shoulder and spit out, 'I don't know, why don't we ask the little rectal-hole dictator herself?'" This time Eric's table erupted in laughter and Bethany Anne just shook her head.

This was the third such party on the actual anniversary of the event, and the team always tried to listen to see where Eric was padding the story and get his story back on track.

Which was to say, somewhere near reality.

Eric put down his beer. "This is the best part, I promise." His table quieted down. "So there was John, dying, knife in his chest, and Bethany Anne was willing to help save him. She drank some blood out of pouches, and then she yanked the knife out while I got the vest and shirt and shit off him. She sliced her wrist and got him to drink her blood, then put some on his chest wound. You know we're connected with an alien now, but back then we didn't have a clue. John was healing from the nanocytes in the blood and Bethany Anne collapsed beside him, spent herself."

Eric looked around and bent forward to his table, lowering his voice as the others leaned in to hear him. "So John woke up and was a little freaked about turning into a vampire. We promised him he wasn't going to, or at least that was what Bethany Anne told us, so then John flops his left arm around and his hand lands on Bethany Anne's chest and he ends up groping the boss." Eyes around the table opened wide, not believing Eric, who put up three fingers. "Scout's honor, no shit. Then Bethany Anne told him, 'I just spent a lot of effort to heal you, Mr. Grimes. If you don't get your hand off my tit, I'm going to waste all that effort when I kill you myself.'"

People started laughing and Eric, smiling widely, put his hand up to quiet them down. "John asked, 'Well, what do I spend the points on for cussing creatively if not to buy a quick feel?' and

Bethany Anne told him, and I'm not kidding, 'John, I have a headache.'"

This time there was no keeping Eric's table quiet when they saw Bethany Anne place her head in her hands as if she was trying to hide.

CHAPTER ELEVEN

<u>Schwabenland, Antarctica</u>

"Is this the right choice, Maria?" Horst asked her.

Maria was listening to those who would decide where they would go. While Maria's decision was accepted as the core desire, the decision about where all of them should go was something that those at the top needed to agree upon. It was larger than just a location. It concerned what would happen to their legacy as well.

Schwabenland would be no more.

Maria looked around the table at the other eight people present. She smiled at them all and gave the tiniest of shrugs. "I cannot be sure, but I can tell you that the decision allows me to sleep at night."

"We left one war to join another," Horst stated. "Ironic, that."

"Were we ever *not* at war, Horst?" she asked. Maria could tell that those with concerns had voted Horst the spokesperson. "We made a deal with the devil to be here. I'm sure he thought once he took care of the world, he would have time to deal with us."

"Then the Americans came," Horst reminded her.

"Yes, they did, and you and the Guards of Freedom fought for our own version of independence, choosing never to accept a world leader over us again."

"And what is changing your mind now?" Horst asked.

Maria looked around the table. "Relations, and time." She turned back to Horst. "Would you want to fight—continue to fight—against those here on Earth? We have been attacked already, and the Etheric Empire is leaving." She pointed up, toward space. "They are leaving to take the fight for Earth's freedom away from here. This makes sense. We have a choice. Never again will we have freedom due to obscurity here. Now we have the opportunity to be welcomed in any country. Not for our bodies," there were a few smiles around the table, "but for our minds, and more importantly, for our technology. But once they have that? Well, we would be irrelevant once again."

"And the Etheric Empire, what do they want us for?" Horst asked. Not in a disrespectful manner, but a firm question nonetheless.

"Actually, nothing." Maria answered, "Our technologies are not as powerful as what they have already. Their people—some of their people—are so advanced by genetic and nanocyte manipulation that they will live to be hundreds of years old."

"I thought Barnabas was already centuries old?" Horst asked.

"He is, Horst. He has lived over ten centuries. If you want to know the measure of evil, he will tell you that he lived it. At one time he felt he was the living embodiment of evil."

"And we would follow such as this?" Cheryl, a woman wearing a faded green dress, asked from her left. Her hair, long and gray, fell past her shoulders. "Can evil redeem itself?"

"That is the existential question, isn't it Cheryl?" Maria queried. "It is not the actions that need to change, since those are imprinted in history and one can only atone for them. No, the question is, can one's soul change?"

"So what is the answer?" Horst demanded.

Maria blew out a breath. "I've come to understand that to answer the question, we need to ask that question of ourselves."

"What? How so?" Horst asked, surprised.

"Because, I've been in contact with the alien TOM. It seems that those who provided me and my sisters with help are not generally considered as wise, caring, and wonderful as we perhaps thought them." She shrugged. "From that perspective, if it is true, we have implemented evil. It was only due to something happening on the Aldebarans' side—what, I don't know—that we didn't finish the plans necessary to have them come here."

"How were we supposed to know?" Cheryl interrupted.

"Is result or intent the deciding factor here?" Maria asked. "Because I understand our intent was correct, but the result might have been the subjugation of Earth had we been successful."

"Why do you believe this alien, TOM?" Horst asked.

"Because I have a soft spot for aliens?" she answered with a smile. "No, I asked him to allow me to speak with the Yollin, Captain Kael-ven, as well. Between the two, they convinced me it is more likely than not."

"How does this tie in with Barnabas?" Cheryl asked.

"When he was 'in his evil mind,' others had killed his spouse. He does not remember that time. After this event he lived as a monk, seeking peace and wisdom away from humanity as much as possible and asking questions incessantly."

"That hasn't changed," Horst muttered.

"No," Maria answered to the amusement of the others. "He still asks a lot of questions, that is true, but he was wise enough to find out if Bethany Anne could contain the beast he fears is still within himself should it become uncaged."

"What happened?" Cheryl asked.

"I understand she knocked him out many times before he realized he should stop asking questions that pissed her off," Maria answered dryly.

"Wow, wish that was possible for me." Horst stared at Maria.

"Bully," she replied.

"Oh, sure, the whole 'weak woman' card." Horst grinned. "This century seems to be much more about gender equality, Maria."

"Well, I'll inform Bethany Anne or one of the other women you wish to work out with them, shall I?"

"Let's not get hasty here. Those are young women, and I'd hate to learn an unfortunate lesson."

"Ageist," Maria retorted.

"I'm allergic to black and blue marks," Horst responded. "They don't heal very quickly anymore."

"Hmmph," Cheryl grumbled. "So you believe that a human can do evil, but without intent it isn't the same?"

Maria nodded. "In this case, yes, but I want to caution you that I feel for those here on Earth and I would try to help our nation, at some level, with our technology."

"What does TQB say about it?" Horst asked.

"They believe it could lead to destabilization between the world powers. However, while TQB is trying to find those that attacked us, they still have not at this point. I would provide the technology transfer with some qualifications that should keep the advance down; to a degree, anyhow. If the people who came after us are not found our country can catch up to the technology, I should hope. Should an alien race of which we are unaware of at this time try to impose their will on the Earth, then I presume those in Germany would share the technology so the world could quickly respond."

Maria shrugged. "Those that wish to remain may stay. Those that wish to go with me to another star system may. Who will go?"

Maria looked around the table and nodded in relief.

Every hand was raised.

. . .

A Dark Field outside Brussels, Belgium

"If you think I'm going to go into the trees with you, Abd, you've been bitten too many times by a camel," Tanya told the man who was trying to coerce her to go for a walk.

Just a little one.

"Abd, stand back," Abdullah ordered as he joined them. Abd made excuses, then went over to the huddle of twenty men waiting and smoking some ten paces away.

"If you were wearing proper clothing this would not happen," Abdullah told her.

"You and I both know that is a lousy excuse. I should be able to walk as naked as I was brought into this world through here unmolested."

"Perhaps that is how it should be, but it is not how it is," Abdullah explained. "When one is stronger, the temptations can be quite difficult to subdue."

"Then perhaps it is a good thing I have a pistol to help me with negotiations, yes?" Tanya asked.

Abdullah looked down and saw her revealing a concealed weapon. "Yes. The cat has claws, I see."

"No, the cat has nine rounds," Tanya replied, "and multiple mags, if necessary, to continue the discussion."

Abdullah looked into the night sky. "When is this magical carpet ride going to get here?"

"He's already up there," Tanya offered. "He's just waiting for me to let him know to land."

Abdullah looked at her. "Why didn't you tell him to land already?"

Tanya took a couple of steps forward and spoke over her shoulder. "Because it would have been easier from up there for him to shoot everyone here if someone was going to be stupid with me."

Tanya told the men to move back or be flattened, and moments later, one of the larger Majestic 12 ships landed silently just meters from them. It stood on four legs, and a ramp lowered from beneath the ship. Two men with weapons exited the craft.

Tyler went to speak with Abdullah and Antony approached Tanya. "Trouble?"

She shrugged. "Nothing I couldn't handle. This isn't my first rodeo, and it would have been more trouble to find another twenty willing participants quickly."

"Understood." He leaned closer. "Just to be clear, they know everyone is getting off and shooting across in space, right? We aren't landing anywhere inside."

Tanya turned toward the twenty men and nodded, whispering, "Everyone understands this will put them in the history books as the first suicide bombers in space for the glory of Allah."

Antony straightened. "Well, they'll be that much closer to heaven when they explode. They don't have bombs on them now, do they?"

Tanya smiled grimly. "No. I explained their stuff wasn't going to work well in outer space."

She turned back to Antony. "I told them our bombs are much better."

New Mexico, USA

One week was how long it took Barnabas to track Abesemmins to DC and the others to follow him back to a location in New Mexico before they lost him when he flew into the desert and disappeared underground.

It made sense, actually. Barnabas and others had decided that the most likely location for the people they were seeking was underground. That said, the site also needed to be in a relatively unpopulated area. However, when you have dozens, if not hundreds, of ways to leave from over two thousand square miles? Trying to pinpoint where they were really hidden boggled the mind.

So, Team BMW came up with a solution that started with a mix of existing drone technology out of Japan and added additional technologies, including self-destruct sequences that would go into effect if the system ever was out of contact with its primary for more than thirty seconds.

It was time.

The dropship Pod, unseen above the clouds, dropped three small dark-gray parent orbs into the night.

They fell three miles before slowing their mad rush to finally hover just inches above the ground. Alone in the night, no humans saw the first orb open and disgorge twelve flying insects.

Made of metal.

After receiving instructions, the insects fluttered to a site that allowed them entrance into the underground cavern system below.

The second and third orbs moved silently in the night. The second stopped five miles south of the first's location and released twelve of its own drones.

The third was three miles to the west and did the same thing.

Each insect drone flew into the caves and mapped the inside with 3D laser technology, uploading the information directly to their parent.

The controlling drone then sent the information to the dropship Pod, which sent the information via the Etheric to ArchAngel.

Before long, thirty-six tiny drones were mapping the caverns in the Dulce Lake region. Occasionally one would have to stop and backtrack back out, and five times the little drones had to leave the cavern they were searching and seek another surface entrance to reenter into the caves and continue their task.

The cavern system, ArchAngel calculated, was huge.

Every fifteen hours the little drones would return to the main Pod for a recharge, then go back into the system again. Occasionally they would get different orders, depending on what Arch-Angel was piecing together.

ADAM was watching the results with interest. If ever an AI could be said to feel emotion, it was happening now.

ADAM was feeling pleasure.

Boston, Massachusetts, USA

Charles nodded to the security officer, then drove past the gate into the large country estate. He didn't recognize this security person, but then again he didn't pay much attention to the security guards anyway.

The only reason he noticed this time was because the guard looked Japanese. A strange occurrence, to be sure, but not out of the realm of possibility.

Charles pulled into the spot marked with a large Cyrillic 'C.' The next two spots were labeled with the letters 'F' and 'D' respectively.

Charles got out of his Range Rover and grabbed his briefcase. The resolution in the Senate to pass electrical power legislation was doing well so far, and should benefit their oil interests. The United Nations was moving forward as well. After closing his door, he walked toward the entrance of the mansion and pressed his hand against the security panel. The lock clicked and he stepped inside, closing the door behind him.

Their security people were responsible for the outside. The whole purpose of the mansion was to keep secrets...secrets he and David and Fred spoke of openly within the walls of this building. They had cleaners come in, and then security swept the house for anything the cleaners might have left behind.

Since the three of them weren't living here, this happened once a month.

He went through the foyer into the bar, set his briefcase down, and quickly made himself a rum and Coke. After hanging his coat on the rack, he grabbed his drink and case and continued down the carpeted hallway into the library.

He stopped at the chessboard and raised an eyebrow. Fred had moved, but it was a strange one. Charles' eyebrows drew together as he studied the board with more focus, trying to fathom the reason for the move. If he didn't know better, he would swear Fred had paid a ringer to play for him.

Charles put down his briefcase and took a sip of his drink, thinking through all the different moves and countermoves. He stood there almost five minutes before he recognized the trap.

He might be in trouble.

Charles frowned. This was too subtle for Fred. Either he had paid someone to help him with this move, or he had gotten lucky and had no idea that twelve steps in the future Charles would be in trouble. He took another sip and moved his Queen to Bishop's three before bending down and picking up his briefcase and walking further into the room. He had almost made it to his chair when he stopped.

Drink halfway up to his mouth, he stared at the dusky-skinned beauty sitting in David's chair. It happened to be facing away from the chessboard, and the back was too high for him to see sooner that someone was occupying it.

Someone who shouldn't be here.

"Who are you?" he asked her.

"Tabitha. Why don't you sit down, Charles? Fred and David have just arrived, and will be joining us shortly."

Charles didn't move. He pointed at Tabitha using the hand with the drink, anger coloring his voice. "You are not supposed to be here. This is private property." He looked around the room to see if anyone else might be hiding.

"Since when do rules mean anything to you, Charles?" Tabitha asked. She stood gracefully and her hand trailed along the back of the leather chair as she walked around it. She was dressed in a black pantsuit with its sleeves slit down the length of the fabric, her tanned arms peeking in and out of view.

Charles could hear his two partners talking to each other when David abruptly changed his tone and spoke louder. "Guard, you are not supposed to be inside this house! I will call and inform your company they will be docked for failure to— Good God, stop pointing that pistol at me!"

"What is the meaning of this?" Fred snapped, and Charles turned to see his partners practically pushed into the room by an Asian security guard who was aiming a pistol at them.

"Seriously, Jun?" Tabitha asked him.

"It was part of the outfit, Kemosabe, and it was easier than listening to their complaints."

Tabitha spoke to the three older men, pointing to their chairs. "Take a seat, gentlemen. You're going to be here a while."

"Why?" David burst out. "You will be arrested and charged with—"

She interrupted, "I'm not one of the three people on trial here, dickwad!"

Fred, his stupefied mind trying to parse the coarse language used by the woman in front of him, turned to Charles.

"Well, Fred, seeing as how we don't have the pistol, why don't we humor the woman?" Charles asked as he took the two steps necessary to get to his chair. He sat down.

The other two men less graciously went to their own chairs and sat. Tabitha put out her hand. "Briefcases, please." The men looked at each other with questions on their faces. When Jun cleared his throat, the three looked disgusted but turned their briefcases over to Tabitha.

She walked back to the table and set them down, then reached to her right and picked up a small diary. "Why don't we start with what you guys have written in this book, shall we?"

"That's personal!" Fred burst out. "Don't you know a diary when you see one?"

we are truly as destitute as this woman says we are, who is going to take care of those families?"

Barnabas turned to Tabitha. "You drained them dry?"

She snorted. "Asshole Response 101, hit them in their pocketbook. ADAM is taking care of the results."

Barnabas nodded.

"What about *our* damned families?" David asked. "Are they not part of your equation? You won't get away with this, either. I don't know how you think you'll walk away from this. Our security gates and these grounds are tracked continuously."

"Yes, and they are all connected on the Internet for downloads. Conversely, that means they are online for uploads, as well," Tabitha replied. "Achronyx took care of your *chiquitito* security system, *Señor.*"

"I'm going to sue your asses into oblivion." Fred pointed at Barnabas, then at Tabitha. "You won't have enough to buy toilet paper to wipe your ass when you shit under a bridge."

Tabitha looked at Barnabas. "How about now?"

Barnabas shook his head and shrugged. "I tried." He looked out through the large window to the trees beyond. "You can call her."

Tabitha closed her eyes as she heard David ask. "Call who?"

"Bethany Anne," Charles answered. "Fred, you are a world-class jackass."

"Why? What's she going to do?" Fred retorted.

"Not helping, idiot," Charles warned.

Fred's chair squeaked. "Bah, these two are just playing good-cop bad-cop. We know Bethany Anne is somewhere off Earth. By the time she can get here, the cops will be swarming this place."

Bethany Anne?

One moment, she replied.

Tabitha kept her eyes closed. She didn't care to see these three assholes any longer.

Okay, done kicking Eric's ass. What's up?

Barnabas has given me permission to ask what you want to do with the three assholes who were behind the attack on the Jaydens?

Little Anne and her family? Bethany Anne's voice came back, going frosty over their mental link.

That's correct.

Where are you? she demanded. Tabitha could almost feel the fire in her eyes as she walked out of wherever she was toward her room.

Boston, Massachusetts, in a private home on wooded property outside of town.

Where is the G'laxix Sphaea?

Right on top of our heads. Well, a few miles above us.

Let me grab Ashur. I'll be there in about... Hold on, I'm figuring... Say ten minutes.

Understood, Tabitha finished.

She opened her eyes to see all four men watching her. "She'll be here in ten."

"Hmph, impossible!" David snorted.

"Not if we have bad intel," Charles sat back in his chair.

Barnabas spoke. "If you believe she is with the large station, you would be right."

"Not that I'm curious, but I'm curious. How do you know this?" Tabitha asked Charles.

"Basing it on the length of time they hadn't seen her," Barnabas answered when none of the men said a word.

The three looked sharply at Barnabas.

Tabitha walked over to the table. "Well, that secret is still a secret, it seems." She picked up the first briefcase. "Wow, talk about old tech." She turned to Barnabas, "Should I pick it?"

"No, you would find the status of their present projects, a few secret files they shouldn't possess, a ham sandwich in David's briefcase, and other various stuff you would expect."

"How the hell do you know that?" David asked.

"He's reading our minds." Charles slumped in his chair and turned to look out the window to the trees beyond. "Checkmate."

"Why are you giving up?" Fred asked. "These two aren't killers, and neither is the woman coming."

Charles looked at Fred. "You need to open your eyes a little more, Fred." He pointed to Tabitha. "She's the one who jumped out of the third-story window in Germany. Remember that video?"

Fred looked at the woman in the attractive pantsuit and then back at Charles. "What of it?"

"She's a modified human, Fred." He pointed at Barnabas. "He's God-only-knows-what, but he's either," Charles pointed to his own head, "reading our damned minds or can see through our briefcases, unless they have some magic trick I can't fathom." He pointed at Jun behind the men. "They have replaced all our security, can travel faster than light somehow to get here from outer space and," he turned to face Barnabas, "how old are you, really?"

There was a pause before Barnabas answered, "A thousand years and then a few."

"Well, shit." Charles muttered. "I hadn't expected that answer."

"How could you?" Barnabas asked. "It's a pretty well-guarded secret."

"Secrets are our trade," Charles replied. "At least, we thought they were."

The men all got lost in their own thoughts for a few minutes.

Quiet enveloped the room, and then a sense of unease permeated the men. The brothers adjusted themselves in their chairs, and Charles started looking around.

"She's here," Tabitha stated. "Vengeance has arrived."

The men, unsettled by Tabitha's comment, looked at each other before turning to the door. They heard footsteps—multiple pairs of them. The first one through the door wasn't human.

It was the biggest damned white German Shepherd any of them had ever seen.

It trotted over to Tabitha and looked up at her until she broke. "Fine, fine, how are you Ashur, besides begging for a head rub?" she asked as she scratched behind his ears. He chuffed to her and she chuckled. "Yeah, the hound finally ran down the foxes, big guy."

Second through the door was a mountain of a man. White, dressed in a black suit with black sunglasses, he had to be damn near six and a half feet tall.

He paused in the doorway, then continued into the room when he was comfortable with the situation.

Then *she* came in. She wasn't what they had expected. She carried herself regally, but she held a sword in her hands. It looked to be generations old, but she carried it like it was a normal part of her life.

Her hands had used it.

The fear the men felt escalated as she drew near them. She stood beside Barnabas and looked the three men over. "Well, my Rangers, it seems the longest open case you've had is now going to close. Well done. Here sit the instigators that paid to have a little girl tied to a bomb in Las Vegas."

Fred started to talk, but she looked at him and pinched her fingers in his direction. Overwhelming fear raced through his body, and it was all he could do to breathe. "Judged!" Her eyes flashed.

"What are you doing to my brother!" David yelled, fear in his voice as he watched his brother's clenched hands pounding on his chair in pain.

Bethany Anne turned and looked David up and down. "Here, I'll show you." She pushed a hand toward him and his body screamed at him to run, to leave, but he couldn't move. His heart raced faster and faster, and he couldn't get enough air. "Judged," she repeated and turned to Charles.

Charles tried to stand up to run, but a hand grabbed his shoulder and shoved him back into his chair. Charles looked up to see the big guard behind him, his dark sunglasses showing Charles only his own reflection.

The brothers were struggling in their chairs, their faces turning blue. "What the hell are you doing?" Charles asked, his voice breaking as he watched his partners.

"Allowing them to die together," Bethany Anne replied. "I've spoken with Barnabas, and all three of you are guilty of things that killed other human beings. You willfully used your power without regard for others, never caring what those in your employ did to accomplish your whims. You have all earned this judgment for many past sins." Charles paled as he watched the twitching of his friends get feebler, the brothers asphyxiating slowly and painfully. He only looked back at her when he realized she was watching him.

And her eyes were glowing red.

She spoke, voice deeper than a moment ago, and he heard it both in his ears and inside his mind. "Charles, you paid those who endangered a little girl in Las Vegas. That was the decision which brought you to this end. You deserved this years ago."

The fear he was feeling became a desire to leave, to escape, but he couldn't. His body was locked in indecision as his mind screamed in fear and chemicals released in his body at a level that should never occur.

Charles struggled, never noticing that Fred and David had stopped moving.

Two minutes later Charles was still, and Bethany Anne stopped *pushing* fear into the man's body.

"You bastards," Bethany Anne spat when she was done. "You fucking camel-sucking jackasses had to try to have it all. This was a peaceful fucking end considering how you should have gone down." She started walking out. "Rangers, you did superbly. Clean up as needed. I'll expect a final report in two days, Barnabas. I've got the president's thing to go to this week."

Barnabas started walking out the door himself as he spoke

back over his shoulder, "Tabitha?"

"Yes?" she called after him.

"I'll expect that report by tomorrow morning." He left the room behind Bethany Anne.

She watched him walk out, her mouth open. "Well, *Gott Verdammt!*" she complained as she put the briefcases next to the three men. "Jun, tell the other Tontos to clean up and put the security people back where we found them. Barnabas' mental commands are going to drop within," she looked at her watch, "twenty minutes."

Jun followed her out. "Yes, Kemosabe. What else do we need to do?"

"Take only what we need, and then find us a place to hole up for the night back in New York. I've got fucking reports to write," she huffed.

New Mexico, USA

The system easily spotted the small flying insect. It allowed it to pass the first checkpoint, but five minutes later when the little bug didn't veer off course the secondary security system shot it out of the air.

It dropped like a rock, landing in a crevice beside a boulder.

The security system confirmed there was no movement in the air and went back to passive mode.

The little drone did not move, but it did send a message to the parent orb that was quickly relayed to the sky, then to outer space.

Drone 012 attacked by a laser emitting on non-customary wavelength. Instructions?

ArchAngel passed the information to the highest general in the Etheric Empire for review.

General Lance Reynolds received the message and smiled.

They had found the bastards.

"That was an awful feeling," Yuko told Akio. She smiled. "I'm glad you're my friend."

"I'm hundreds of years old, Yuko. Understand when I say I am very glad you call me friend."

Yuko put her head against him. "I don't deserve you guys, you know that?"

Akio put his arm around her as they made their way up the round staircase. "And that is precisely why you do."

This time Akio was ready for Yuko to stop when she saw how packed the viewing deck was.

Everyone was waiting for her and Akio to join them, and Yuko couldn't stop the tears from falling. She put her hand up to her face to catch the tears but Gabrielle suddenly was beside her, wiping them with a tissue.

"Bethany Anne told me to be ready, but damn, girl! You were supposed to make it at least five steps into the club for me to win."

Yuko choked a laugh as she took the tissue and dabbed at her eyes. "Who won?"

"ADAM, that AI silicon sonofabitch," Gabrielle spat. "I'm out two ounces of gold, too. Greedy bastard."

ADAM? Yuko called.

>>**YES?**<<

You bet on me?

>>**Of course.**<<

But... Yuko didn't have anything to say.

>>**I had to have money or else I couldn't give you my present.**<<

You got me a present?

>>**Yes. Bethany Anne told me if it was to be from me I had to make the money myself, so I've been doing that.**<<

What do you need money for? Yuko asked. *You don't owe me anything.*

>>I might not owe you anything, but I wanted to give you something. Now enjoy the party.<<

Yuko took a step onto the viewing deck and greeted her friends.

Akio was talking with Darryl and Scott when he felt her presence. Turning around, he bowed to his Queen. "Got a minute?" she asked.

"Yes, my Queen." he replied, and she put a hand on his shoulder. "We'll be right back," she told the guys, and they disappeared.

"Now that," Scott observed to Darryl, "I'd like to figure out how to do."

"I understand it takes a certain amount of something you don't have," Darryl told his friend.

"Really?" Scott turned to him. "What?"

Darryl patted Scott's shoulder. "Intelligence."

Bethany Anne and Akio arrived in one of the bar's private rooms. It was locked from both sides so no one would accidentally venture in while Bethany Anne was transporting back and forth. While she made an effort to look before she arrived, it was always better to be as safe as possible.

"Yes, my Queen?" Akio asked her.

"How is Yuko?"

"She has made her decision, but it is still painful when friends leave."

Bethany Anne nodded. "I understand. Are you okay with staying?"

Akio nodded, "I am good with this, my Queen. It isn't like I can't speak with you," he tapped his head, "if I must."

"True, but remember… Due to the distance, it's very draining."
She put a hand on his shoulder. "He will be back, Akio. I don't
know when, but probably not soon. Please take care of my people
on Earth as they do whatever the hell they do. Continue the
responsibilities of the Queen Bitch in my absence. Are we clear?"

"*Hai*, we are clear, my Queen," he replied. Then, looking into
her eyes, he smiled. "You brought honor back, when I felt there
was none left. I and my men will do what you ask until our dying
breath or he returns."

"I'll be back, whether it's a hundred years or a thousand," she
promised. "If I'm not dead, I'll be back when this is finished."
Bethany Anne took her hand off his shoulder and walked to a
small dresser at the side of the room. Opening the top drawer,
she pulled out a sword in a sheath, and after closing the drawer,
she turned around.

"You are my Elite, my Bitch on Earth. Take this sword as
evidence of my faith in you, and wield it in my absence. You are
my representative. Your actions bring me honor, your respect
brings me honor. Take it now and know you have my complete
trust, Akio."

Akio pursed his lips and bowed. "I understand I may not
refuse," he held out his hands, "so I accept my Queen."

Bethany Anne smiled and put the sword in his hands. "Good,
'cause I really don't want to have to fight you to make you take it."

Akio smiled. "That would not be respectful, my Queen." Then
he grinned. "It wouldn't feel good either."

Bethany Anne laughed. "You know, I think being around
William has helped loosen you up a little, Akio." She thought
about it for a second. "Not much, but a little."

"Yes," he smiled as they headed toward the door, "William is
an interesting experience, my Queen."

"I've put this off as long as I can." She sighed. "Now comes the
worst part of the evening: I have to tell Yuko goodbye."

CHAPTER FOURTEEN

"So, I was shot, blood gushing out of me," Yuko listened for the umpteenth time as William related his story of getting shot in Japan, "when Akio comes and just slays the guys who did this to me. I'm foggy, fading in and out of consciousness, and I see Akio, red eyes blazing as he kneels and I bravely bite on a piece of leather as he jams in his claws to pull out the slugs—"

"He fainted," Akio stated from behind William.

William turned around and looked down at Akio, who had Bethany Anne behind him. "Hey, you are absolutely messing up a good story with the facts. Didn't Bobcat and I teach you better than that?"

"Right," Akio deadpanned. "Well, I'll just switch places with Yuko here." He reached out and gently pulled Yuko toward him, then he did some sort of trick where one second he was behind her and the next she was behind him. "My Queen?"

Bethany Anne winked, then the ladies were gone.

Akio turned back around to those listening to William. "I understand I looked like this?" Akio asked, and willed his eyes to go red. When he spoke his voice was a little harsher. "Do continue, brother!"

Those listening to William took an involuntary step backward, but leaned forward again to listen to the story, anxious to see what happened next as Akio helped William tell the tale.

If not exactly the truth.

Bethany Anne and Yuko appeared in her suite, and Yuko looked around. "Oh!"

Ashur chuffed from the bed and Yuko walked over to him. "I'll miss you too, fluffy one!" She grabbed him around the neck. "You protect our Queen, all right?" Ashur whined and Yuko laughed, letting him go. "Yes, I know that is an impossible task, but you are the right dog for the mission, yes?"

Ashur chuffed again and Yuko rubbed his head. "I thought so."

Yuko turned around to see Bethany Anne dabbing at her eye with a tissue. "Don't, Bethany Anne! You're going to make me mess up my makeup worse."

Bethany Anne opened her arms, and Yuko stepped forward to hug her. "You know we're all going to miss you, right?" Yuko nodded and said something muffled in Bethany Anne's chest. "Especially ADAM."

Yuko looked up. "Hey, ADAM! What was it you wanted to give me?"

"Ah." Bethany Anne stepped back. "I was wondering if you were going to keep it a secret, ADAM."

ADAM's voice came from Bethany Anne's bathroom. "I had to use it as a way to help Yuko attain equilibrium, and, well, Gabrielle ratted me out."

Yuko leaned to her left to look around Bethany Anne, who was blocking her view of the bath. "ADAM?"

Yuko heard movement, and then he appeared. Yuko moved out from behind Bethany Anne, who stepped aside.

"ADAM?" Yuko asked, confused. "This isn't possible, is it?"

"No," the android agreed. "You are hearing me speak from this android. I have been working on this gift for a year."

Yuko looked up at Bethany Anne, who smiled. "He had to generate the funds," Bethany Anne told her, then added, "Legally."

"Yes," the little android agreed. "It was that requirement which took me a little longer."

"He's..." Yuko reached out and felt the body. It was metal, and the unit didn't try to act like a human. "Beautiful."

The little android put his hand up to gently touch Yuko's. "Thank you."

ADAM's voice switched to coming out of the room's speakers. "Adam Nacht, say hello to Yuko."

The android faced Yuko and its mouth, animated to some degree, spoke. "Hello, Yuko. I am Adam Nacht, the Entity Intelligence who will be working with you."

Yuko looked at Bethany Anne. "His name is Adam?"

Bethany Anne smiled gently. "His name is whatever you decide to call him. Once you change it, the EI is forever that name."

Yuko turned back to the android. "Can you turn around?" The EI turned easily and Yuko sought the seams that must occur in his body. "What is he made out of?"

"Well, He is a synthesis of human metals and Yollin alloys which we were able to forge out here in the asteroid."

"How?' Yuko asked, still feeling the seamless body.

"With a lot of help," ADAM told her. "A lot of friends at the party helped."

"I'm going to have to tell them all thank you." Tears smeared her makeup.

"What would you like my name to be?" the EI asked. "I can be male, female, or gender neutral."

Yuko thought about it. "Well, ADAM is ADAM to me, and it feels weird to have a boy as a friend, so..."

Yuko held out her hand. "Hello, Eve. My name is Yuko, and you have no idea how pleased I am to meet you."

Bethany Anne handed Yuko clean tissues after she finished shaking hands with the shorter android.

"Are there special care instructions that come along with her?" Yuko asked as she tried to clean up her mascara.

"No, I have a multi-century power supply," Eve answered.

"Ah, I get it—ADAM and Eve." ADAM laughed.

"Interesting," Bethany Anne murmured. "Eve was begotten from ADAM, and that's true here, as well." Bethany Anne dabbed at her eyes one last time. "Yuko, I have a few words to say before I go. I have to go meet with a bunch of sticks-in-the-mud about stuff they want that I won't give them."

Yuko turned to Bethany Anne.

"First, you can't police the world. Don't try. Whatever they do, let them! Your responsibility is to the UnknownWorld. Akio is responsible for taking care of any Forsaken, and you are responsible for taking care of those who would honor Michael's family or me."

Yuko nodded her understanding.

"So, be strategic and be smart. I know you already understand how to rely on Akio and the team, but you are getting older and wiser yourself. You have good intuition, so remember to use it. Continue with your strength and martial training. It will come in handy. So," she nodded at Eve, "will she. We have two EI containers running her intelligence. She is the closest to an AI we have."

"Perhaps one day she will be a true AI," ADAM added. "I've calculated the computing power, and it is within the realm of possibility."

"Truly?" she asked. She looked at Eve, who returned her look. "What would it take?"

"That is something you will need to figure out," Bethany Anne replied. "ADAM has placed a huge amount of information in the

EI for you to review on this subject. It could take multiple life-times to go through and master all of it."

Yuko opened one arm and Eve walked over and leaned into her, hugging her gently. "Oh my..." Yuko squeezed the android and smiled. "At least I can't hurt you."

"That is true," Eve agreed. "Not much can."

"Remember, Yuko." Bethany Anne was watching them. "Be strategic with your moves, be smart, and hide rather than show yourself. Be the wind that is whispered in the leaves, a name, a phantom. Exist to bring order and protection, but try to stay hidden to the masses. Your primary objective is to be there for Michael when he arrives. When that happens, Eve will contact us. Be there for my people in the UnknownWorld. Use the tech-nology we've left you to watch as much as you can, but you can't protect everyone. God knows I've tried and failed."

Yuko nodded, understanding her orders.

"I've got to get back to the *ArchAngel* and change, and get down to Earth. Are you sure you want to age?"

"For now, I need to. My parents would not understand if I did not age as they get older. I would not have them wonder."

"I understand. We've enhanced you as much as we can until they are no longer with us, then. We have left as much enhanced nanocytes as we can provide. Use it rather sparingly, okay?"

Yuko nodded.

"All right, one last hug. Then I can take you back to the party, but I'm afraid Eve will have to take the tram."

"That's okay. I like the tram," Eve chirped. "I'll meet you at All Guns Blazing if that is fine with you, Yuko?" The little android stopped and waited for permission.

"Yes, that's fine." Yuko answered. "Wait, how do we communicate?"

We communicate the same way you do with ADAM. Eve's voice, now tilting toward the feminine, echoed in Yuko's ears.

Yuko stared at Eve. "This is so cool, ADAM! I cannot thank you enough!"

"It's what friends do. We take care of each other."

So, ADAM, you going to tell Yuko that Eve is a protection android?"

>>I think there is only one way to answer that, Bethany Anne.<<

Oh? How is that?

>>Hell, no!<<

Bethany Anne schooled her face, fearing she would snicker and give away her communication with ADAM.

"Okay, my Japanese princess, time to get you back to the party, and me on my way to another boring meeting with stuffy old people."

Yuko went to Bethany Anne and hugged her. "Bethany Anne, you have given me two things I would never have had otherwise: a true friend in ADAM, and an opportunity to help my country. We might be staying below the radar, but those who need to know we exist... Well, we will find them, my Queen."

Bethany Anne hugged her back. "It's time."

They disappeared.

Belgium

"Abdullah," Tanya began as she sat in the small coffee shop. He sat down, putting his coffee to the side. "Do you believe we are ready?"

"Yes, all is in place. If you hadn't told us, we would not know an event was occurring." The man took a sip of his coffee.

Tanya looked around the coffee shop. "They're trying to keep the meeting a secret. It's a last-ditch effort to persuade TQB to listen to them and share their technology."

"I hate their leader as much as anyone in the world," Abdullah countered, "but in her position I wouldn't share either. It doesn't take much intelligence to agree there isn't a government to be trusted."

"Except yours?" Tanya asked.

Abdullah shrugged. "I am a leader who enjoys the fight. The fight is here, yes?" He took another sip before setting his coffee down. "Perhaps when I was a little younger, full of what you call piss and vinegar, yes?" Tanya nodded. "Well, in those times I believed more in the prophecies than perhaps I do now."

"What's different now?" Tanya asked. Her voice was curious for once.

"Now it is about making sure my people have space and opportunity. It is not only America who has had religious people trying to use their beliefs to run others' lives. My people have dealt with it for centuries. Just look at how advanced we were a long time ago, and look at us now."

Abdullah flicked his hand, the disgust on his face passing like a bird flying across a yard.

"Now, most of our countries are held by those who would be the next Mohammad or the next Caliph. If not that, then they are ruled by military dictators who don't sleep easy at night for keeping my people down under the threat of death, or kings who do the same thing but are more legitimate in the world's eyes."

Tanya hated to admit it, but she was starting to respect this man.

"What do you hope to accomplish?" Tanya asked him. "You have what, two hundred fighters?"

Abdullah smiled grimly. "Perhaps we were not as upfront with you as we might have been. We have over five hundred men for this operation. You have provided the perfect chance for us to ambush many influential people. Not only TQB's leader, who we want to hit, but the ex-President of the US will be there, right?" Tanya nodded. "Plus maybe three other significant country representatives, and over forty businessmen and other dignitaries. It will be good to take down the ex-President. Perhaps it

161

will be a bigger benefit to us that *he* dies. Most of the people in the villages don't know or care about Bethany Anne."

"We certainly do," Tanya interrupted.

"Don't worry, Ms. Tanya-without-a-last-name," Abdullah replied. "The TQB leader is wanted by people high in many freedom fighter organizations for the raids her people have executed. She will be killed, certainly, but for the rest of those who feel like the Americans have cheated them killing the president is the bigger win."

Tanya nodded. Bethany Anne being killed was all that mattered to her.

If an American ex-President needed to be sacrificed? Well, it would only drum up support for a stronger military in the US. Her team would then have opportunities when it came time for advanced weapons sales.

She was sure that when the technology Majestic 12 had created over the decades was shared, any questionable methods to procure it would be swept under the rug.

"What about air support?" Abdullah asked.

"We brought in all the SAMs you gave us," Tanya replied. "How you disperse them is up to you."

"Is there any additional technology you can offer?" Abdullah asked.

Yes, she thought, *but no fucking way are you getting it. We've had our asses handed to us doing that before.*

She shook her head. "No, nothing we can give you without risking the whole operation. The energy requirements are pretty substantial, so it wouldn't take too much of a sweep to find them. Our efforts tend to be aimed at spaceships, not little ships zipping around the city."

"Too bad. You know TQB will have backup, yes?"

"That's why the SAMs are here. We outfitted a few with enhanced seek-and-destroy targeting. Otherwise, the chance of those things hitting TQB ships would have been about zero."

Abdullah flipped his hand over and back, twice. "It is in the Prophet's hands at that point. We are to stand there and aim, then click the buttons while bullets seek our lives. If he chooses it, the missiles will hit the enemy's ships."

He raised the coffee to his lips. "Of course, if the missiles have better tracking solutions before we fire? Well, that is just advance preparation on the Prophet's part, I believe."

A small curve graced Abdullah's lips as he took a sip.

CHAPTER FIFTEEN

Geneva, Switzerland

Anna Elizabeth slid her feet into the high heels she had purchased expressly for this evening. She had worked for Bethany Anne's company for over three years, and she'd been promoted twice.

One of them had been into the negotiations group.

It had been a surprise to Anna to find out that Bethany Anne no longer owned the parent company. When she first found out she was concerned, and had gone to go speak with Amanda in HR to find out what was going to happen.

For a moment Amanda had looked at her with a blank expression.

"Blackballed," Anna reminded her, pointing to herself. "Remember?"

"Oh!" Amanda responded. "That was taken down when we hired you, didn't you know?" Anna didn't. "Oh, yes," Amanda confirmed, but pulled up the necessary screen to look again. "For us to hire you and for it not to have been a problem, your name had to come off the list. So when the bosses' boss…"

"Bethany Anne," Anna supplied.

"Yes," Amanda pushed up her glasses to peer at her computer. "When she had me hire you, I'm sure she spoke with whomever had put your name on the list and convinced them to take it off."

Anna winced internally. Whoever had blackballed her would have been screwed if they hadn't removed her name. Bethany Anne, as she was aware, took care of her people.

Tonight, however, Anna Elizabeth had a chance to pay Bethany Anne back and ask her if the option to emigrate was still open.

She slipped on the second shoe and stood up to look in the mirror, then turned around and looked over her shoulder.

Yes, the dress looked very good.

She stepped to the closet and grabbed a coat. While it was in the low fifties Fahrenheit during the days, it approached freezing at night and there was a chance of rain.

She had just snagged her purse from the bar when her doorbell rang. She walked over and looked through the peephole.

Holy Crap! She barely saw his chin, but she knew who was on the other side of the door. She opened it and smiled at a man she admired.

"Good evening, my name is—" he started to say, but she interrupted.

"John Grimes!" Anna blurted. She looked into his eyes. "My God, you are so much bigger in person!" She clapped her hand over her mouth, her eyes wide, and her voice came out muffled. "I'm so sorry, that was so rude of me."

John smiled and shrugged. "I'm American. We're good with compliments." John moved aside as Anna stepped out of her apartment and turned to lock the door. "Besides," he added, "Jean isn't here to take offense on my behalf."

"I blame the calendar."

They walked down the hallway to meet Bethany Anne. John's soft laughter lingered in the air as they turned the corner.

Bethany Anne's foot tapped on the deck. They were in one of the posh new Executive Pods, and with seating for ten it didn't lack for comfort.

What it *did* lack was the ability to just make the whole night go away. These stupid meetings went nowhere. The sycophantic suck-ups wanted stuff she wouldn't part with. Sometimes, she was just too nice to friends.

>>**John is signaling and we're going back down.**<<
Good.

She had tried to speak with the two Guardians up front, but apparently Peter had been telling stories and she couldn't get them to yank the sticks out of their asses long enough to chill a little and talk with her.

She was going to have to find that little toadstool and see what lies he had been concocting lately.

Seconds later the door cracked open and Anna Elizabeth stood there transfixed, her eyes alight with the wonder of the Pod coming out of the sky, Bethany Anne was sure.

"Well, come on in! It isn't very warm out there," Bethany Anne told her.

"Oh!" Anna accepted John's help getting in. The Pod stayed a foot off the ground. "Sorry, it's just so weird seeing a big ship come out of the sky without any sound. It was hard to see, even though John pointed it out as you guys arrived."

John got in and shut the door.

"That's by design," Bethany Anne inserted, "but let's not talk about this stuff. Let's talk about you!"

"Me?" Anna asked. "I'm kind of boring."

"Says the cute young woman in her... Oh my *God*, those are beautiful!" Bethany Anne exclaimed as she looked at Anna's shoes. "Manolo Blahniks?"

Anna turned her foot sideways. *"Yes!"* she practically squealed. "I got these last weekend. Do you like them?"

"If I didn't like you so much I would mug you for those." Bethany Anne looked up at Anna. "What's your shoe size?"

Anna looked back. "Five and a half, why?"

"Bethany Anne," John snickered, "is thinking of acquiring them."

"You want them?" Anna asked, confused.

"John, don't be an ass," she told him and then turned to Anna. "I'm like any woman. I see a pair of shoes that are beautiful…"

Anna laughed. "I never knew you had a shoe obsession."

"Oh, it might be a well-kept secret," John offered, "but Bethany Anne and Imelda Marcos have a few things in common."

"All right." Bethany Anne turned to John. "You mention me and Imelda Marcos together one more time, Mr. Grimes, and I'll make you pay next time we practice together."

"Boss, be reasonable," John argued. "You have whole shipping containers of shoes you haven't opened yet. The last three years of entire lines from over—what, seventy designers?"

"You have shipping containers of shoes?" Anna asked.

"It's not like that," Bethany Anne started, then stopped herself. "You know what, it's exactly like that." She flung a hand out toward the window. "How am I supposed to know how long it's going to take to save this place? I need to know that I always have a new pair of shoes in case the latest meeting goes bad. It helps my mental disposition."

"Shipping containers. I heard that right, yes?" Anna asked again.

"Five," John clarified. "Two pairs of each style in her size." He grinned and winked at his boss.

"Hey!" Bethany Anne retorted. "I'm not the only one. Gabrielle has two containers herself, and let's not discuss how many containers of guns and shit you and the other guys are bringing along, especially when your woman has made half that shit you bought useless."

"Whoa!" John put up his hands. "Don't be dissin' the firepower. It's a therapeutic release to feel the guns kick and smell the gunpowder after you shoot."

"Yeah." Bethany Anne sat back in her seat further, crossing her arms over her chest. "So is the smell of the leather, the curve of the front of the shoe, and the height of the heels."

Anna gazed back and forth between them as she tried one last time.

"Shipping containers from container ships? Those are the ones you have?"

John looked at Anna and his hands opened, all ten fingers splayed. He silently mouthed, "Tens of thousands of pairs!"

Bethany Anne, although looking out the window, lifted her hand and flipped John off to the laughter of everyone in the Pod.

You better pray to Saint Payback-is-a-Bitch, she thought to herself, *because your time is coming.*

The ex-President and his security, David, waited in the dark next to the limousine near their plane. The ex-President was looking into the night sky. "You ever looked up into the sky, knowing there were aliens out there going about their business day to day just like you?"

David, who was keeping a watch around the area, answered, "Not too much, sir. I have to admit it was a weird feeling meeting the Yollins on the *ArchAngel*."

"Yes, the Yollins... It helps a little to know they also fear the Kurtherians." He looked at David. "At least TQB is not fighting figments of their imaginations."

David shrugged. "Not always sure I agree with their methodology, sir. Those decisions are above my pay grade."

"I get it, David," he answered and looked back up to the sky. He might have been out of office, but one didn't leave behind the feeling of responsibility as easily as taking off a coat.

David reached up to his ear. "We have incoming."

"Where?"

David turned and pointed to the south. "That direction. TQB informed me and traffic control, who happen to be bitching that they can't see them."

Just then there was the tiniest amount of thrum one felt but couldn't hear and the TQB Executive Pod came swooping in, making a tight circle before coming to rest near the limousine. David watched as the door opened and John Grimes stepped out. He checked the area before he allowed Bethany Anne and one more woman out.

The door closed, and the Pod lifted back into the night sky and disappeared.

The ex-President watched it go as they walked up to him. "Where are they going?"

"Back up to *ArchAngel*," Bethany Anne explained. "Good to see you again."

The ex-President greeted her with a smile and a hug. "Thank you for this."

"Yeah, you owe me," she agreed, and they separated. "I'm dreading this like a trip to the dentist."

"You don't need to go to a dentist," John observed as he opened the door to the limousine.

"I don't need to do this either," she retorted. "Before we go, let me introduce Anna Elizabeth Hauser to you guys. She works in negotiations for her company, and has worked for me in the past."

The ex-President put out his hand. "Pleased to meet you, Ms. Hauser." He shook her hand before waving the ladies into the car. "Ladies first."

"Thank you," Anna replied and ducked her head to enter. Bethany Anne followed.

He slid in next, allowing the two security guards to get in last, David with them and John up front. The ex-President looked at Bethany Anne. "So, you really are going to give this a shot?"

"You mean because I dragged Anna along on this?" she asked. "Yeah, I'm not going to waste my time on the infinitesimally small chance it would work without at least giving it the old college try."

"Really? What college?" he asked, and grinned at her. They felt the car pull out.

"Damn, you people never quit, do you?" she asked him, laughing. "Or is it the bounty?"

"Oh, the bounty of course," he replied. "It's what, up to fifteen million now?"

>>**Twenty-two and a half million.**<< ADAM supplied.

"It's over twenty million, now," she corrected him.

David whistled but didn't say anything as he looked out the window.

"We can split the money," he told her. "I mean, ten million just to whisper a name to me?" His smile grew wider. "Imagine the—"

"Bullshit that would happen to anyone who used to know me?" She looked at him with a frank expression this time. "I moved a person I knew from my past twice already before she finally decided to just take me up on my offer to emigrate."

"That is true." His smile faded. "They would chase anyone who knew you."

"More than that. Depending on the country, 'interrogate' is the proper term."

"Unfortunately too true," he agreed. "By the way, China wasn't invited to this, seeing as how you still have frosty relations with them."

"Those bastards are lucky I haven't flattened their leadership and put a new set in place."

"Some are wondering why that hasn't occurred yet."

"Because the computer calculations of the potential social issues brought about by a decapitation of the Chinese government isn't worth the enjoyment I would derive from it."

"So sleeping at night wouldn't bother you?" he asked.

Bethany Anne looked at him. "When you had to send men into battle on foreign soil, did you worry about the wives of the soldiers they killed?"

"Some, I'll admit," he shrugged, "but they chose to pick up arms against us."

"Same thing. Just because they don't have a gun, their political games and what they allow in the name of their country is on the heads of the politicians. The buck, or yuan, stops there."

He nodded his understanding.

The hotel was over three hundred years old. With the spires lit up against the night sky and a gold angel statue at one corner, the hotel looked like a small five-story castle. The car was stopped at the gated entrance, and then they were allowed into the inner courtyard and stopped a few feet from the front doors. The back passenger-side door was opened and David got out. John exited from the front seat next to the driver, and knocked on the roof of the car.

The ex-President exited next, and then Bethany Anne. Anna came out last, and all three were swept inside quickly. As they walked through the inside to a ballroom at the back of the hotel, Bethany Anne was surprised to see a very modern interior compared to the outside of the building.

They even had a bar with purple and green furniture, which was not what she was expecting.

They passed through the more public area, and their rush slowed to a normal pace. Anna Elizabeth started cataloging who she saw and who looked like they had the right intensity for the evening.

Bethany Anne glanced sideways and noticed Anna already had her game on and was analyzing the people in the room as they were announced.

Damn, this woman might make the evening interesting after all.

"Wow, she brings a woman with her to this event?" Sophia whispered to her friend Emma. The ladies, wives of business leaders, often met and gossiped in the corner as each new person arrived at these meetings.

"Yeah, but do you see her security guard?" Emma asked, her eyes going up and down the tall man's body. "Makes you wonder why she's here tonight."

"Because *she* is the woman of the evening, Emma!" Sophia hissed back, only slightly surprised Emma didn't know what the TQB CEO looked like.

Emma was in her own little world.

The operative word, Sophia thought, *was "little."* She swore to her husband that Emma's intelligence could fit inside a tennis ball and have room for nine identical sisters, but at events like this she could be depended upon to provide the evening's entertainment.

Like right now.

Emma kept whispering, "I swear, I would be down on him like a stripper on a pole. No, down like ice cream at a Weight Watchers party. Hmm, maybe down like a case of beer at a frat party." She kept trying new phrases to see which one fit the best.

Sophia looked at her friend, curious. "When was the last time you were at a frat party?"

"What?" Emma looked at her friend, trying to catch up with her question. "Oh, last fall. Took a wrong turn right into a hell of a night. Let me tell you," Emma winked at her, "when they yell 'cougar,' it's a good thing." Sophia snorted.

The two women went back to watching the new arrivals.

"Bethany Anne?" John whispered.

"Ummhmmm," she answered, just as quietly.

"Promise me you won't pass what those two were saying on to Jean?" he asked, while he searched the room for any problems.

"Quid pro quo, Mr. Grimes."

Dammit. He pressed his lips together. *She was going to negotiate this with him.* Fortunately, the first two men joined Bethany Anne and the ex-President and drew them into a conversation. John knew that meant she would stay quiet until they concluded the negotiations.

Before too long Anna stepped into the conversation, asking the business leaders questions about their companies, and within two minutes she had them whimpering, begging to leave the conversation. It took little time before it was obvious these two were puffed-up men whose businesses were hopelessly left behind.

As they left, Anna whispered to Bethany Anne they had probably pulled strings to get into this event. The old hands had allowed those two to go first. It was going to set the mood for the rest of the evening.

Anna had asked relevant questions, instead of Bethany Anne just biting their heads off. She said she saw more men taking their last sips before heading in their direction.

John looked at his watch. It had been over an hour of boring conversations and another two hours to go. Anna had been superb, and Bethany Anne was actually enjoying herself. When those she was negotiating with left, Anna would give Bethany Anne an update on her thoughts and the two would bet on who would approach next.

Occasionally David and John would exchange comments and a few people came up and spoke with the ex-President, but he was really being dragged along in the wake of these two women tonight.

The ex-President found he was enjoying his evening as well.

A couple times he wanted to tell individuals to go away, since he was trying to listen to the women speaking to someone else.

Then the dim but unmistakable staccato firing of weapons could be heard and John, David, and Bethany Anne all turned toward the entrance to the ballroom. Women started screaming, and more than a couple of men started yelling.

Four men from inside the room started running toward the door, two stopping and two continuing on past.

David looked around. "Sir, we need you back in the corner. There are windows in here!"

Bethany Anne's lips pressed together and John put an arm around her and Anna, pulling them toward the wall as people freaked all around them.

"*Gott Verdammt*," Bethany Anne's voice came out of John's chest. He had picked her up and held her close, and her face was planted in his jacket.

John set the two women down and turned around. Bethany Anne and Anna both rearranged their clothes as he looked toward the entrance.

Someone outside yelled they were losing the front door.

"Go, John!" Bethany Anne called, and pointed toward the doors. "We have Pods getting prepped to drop!"

John pulled a pistol and offered it to her, but she ignored it. "I'm armed!" she yelled and then pushed him. "Now fucking *go* already!"

He nodded and turned to David. "You got them both?" David nodded sharply and John ran full-tilt, most people not believing what they saw as he headed toward the front of the hotel.

Bethany Anne looked at the stained-glass windows and frowned. She could depart, but where would that leave most of the others?

"Terrorists," John told her using her implanted ear receiver.

Well, that settled it. When was she going to get a chance like this again?

CHAPTER SIXTEEN

John raced into the hallway, the doors slamming open as he rushed through hoping no one was on the other side.

Except... Sonofabitch! Fucking terrorists. He clicked his microphone. "Terrorists." Pulling his other Dukes special, he set the power to four. He didn't want to worry about who was on the other side of the person he shot.

These pistols were slightly different than her earlier versions. These had larger rods that allowed for mushrooming, like hollow points, when they hit, causing those he shot to feel the concussive damage at lower velocities.

Like right now.

As he came out of the doors, bullets were stitching the carpet in his direction. He twisted, throwing himself to the left and looking hard over his right shoulder. His arms helped speed up the twist, getting him out of the way of the bullets that tracked past him and into the frame of the doors behind him.

John kept his eyes on the three men down the hallway as he twisted. Aiming both pistols, he fired.

He hit the far-right shooter in his shoulder, splattering the man behind him with blood—not that he cared. John's third shot went through that guy's nose and took half his cranium out. The guy on the far-left took two to the chest, thrown backward as the slug's momentum carried him along when they ripped into him like a freight train.

John's body slammed into the left wall, arresting his movement, and he bounced off and landed in a crouch. Firing slowed for a moment, and John ran toward the front of the building.

The beautiful stained-glass window on the far-left side of the room, away from where they stood, shattered as bullets pelted the ceiling inside. Women screamed and men turned toward the new threat.

David turned to look and saw Bethany Anne turn in the direction of the front door again.

"Stay here, Anna!" Bethany Anne told her, and kicked off her heels. Damn! Where were her boots when she needed them?

A female's voice echoed in David's mind. *If it looks like she's going to leave, shoot her.*

"What?" Anna yelled, "Why can't I go with you?"

If it looks like she is going to leave, shoot her.

"Because you aren't me," Bethany Anne replied. "I've got what it…"

Excruciating pain slammed into Bethany Anne's back.

Five Black Eagles screamed down from the *ArchAngel*, itself descending lower into the stratosphere.

"Black Eagle One, one minute from touchdown…"

"We got fire, we got fire!" Black Eagle Two shouted over the intercom.

Black Eagle One called, "Sum-bitch! They're coming right at

us, guys. Break, break, break. Somebody has been studying, and we got unfriendlies. Take your course, lose our friends, and come back. ArchAngel, need a little support here!"

All five Black Eagles turned and raced in separate directions as twelve surface-to-air missiles streaked up from the city below.

Down on the ground there were shouts of glee. Those who had the shoulder-mounted rocket launchers laughed and high-fived their buddies when the SAMs took off in separate directions, obviously following the five retreating Pods.

John was racing toward the entrance when he heard the rush of men coming through the front door, so he raised the power of his Dukes to six.

He didn't think there was anyone behind those coming in his direction he had to worry about.

John careened into the lobby and started laying waste to the men heading toward him.

Those who would be guards were all on the floor, bodies bleeding out what remained of their lives on the tiled floors that others had walked for hundreds of years.

The man closest to John's head exploded when John's first shot hit him between the eyes. Before any of the other terrorists could react, John shot two others in their chests, spraying those behind with blood and gore.

John was just getting started. By the time the first gun's bullets erupted from the muzzle, John had already cleared half—about twelve—of the men in this second wave.

But the damned terrorists were flowing in like floodwaters.

"Sonofabitch!" Next time they told him he couldn't have any grenades he was going to tell them to go fuck themselves.

John cranked the power up to eight and bodies started flying backward as he placed his shots carefully, trying to use the exploding bodies as a beaver would use trees to create a dam to slow the stream.

Where the fuck were all these assholes coming from, anyway? Was there a ten-for-one special on terrorists in Belgium this week?

He took two more shots before Bethany Anne's scream of pain hit him.

Anna shrieked as David raised his gun to shoot Bethany Anne, who was lying on the ground, a second time. Anna jumped him, beating him on the head and ripping at his hair. She was too incoherent to make sense, but Anna's tears flowed down her face as she tried to rip David's eyes with her nails.

David stumbled backward under the weight of the woman as he tried to block her. Finally he put his pistol under her left breast and pulled the trigger twice.

"NOOOO!" screamed someone behind the bitch as Anna's struggling stopped and she collapsed to the floor.

David looked into the flaming red eyes of the woman he had just shot in the back, which were fixed on him and promised him pain beyond imagination.

The Devil herself had risen! David aimed his SA XD-S right at her face and pulled the trigger.

Click.

Oh shit!

He pulled the trigger repeatedly. *Click. Fuck!* He threw the gun at her and she slapped it out of the air.

David ran out of time when the red-eyed demon with talons for fingers stabbed his chest and squeezed his heart. "I'm done with you, you useless degenerate whoring sack-sniffing forsaken fucks!" David's body had barely hit the floor when Bethany Anne, her wrist slit, was forcing blood into Anna's mouth. *"DRINK,*

GODDAMMIT!" she screamed at the woman, whose eyes were losing the will to live.

"I'm not losing another fucking friend to this useless pile of self-serving shit bags. *DRINK!*" Bethany Anne pulled on the Etheric. "*LIVE, DAMN YOU!*" she shrieked, and jolted Anna with Etheric energy. Anna's body spasmed.

"Look out!" the ex-President screamed, and Bethany Anne heard a pistol go off behind her.

She bit off a curse and looked to see what was happening. The ex-President was trying to shoot men coming through the window.

He had been a better president than he was a marksman.

BETHANY ANNE!

I got this, John**, she sent. **Stay up front if it's bad.

It's a fucking tidal wave of terrorists, he replied.

Good. When I finish here I'll fuck them up over there.

What?

Anna breathed in heavily and Bethany Anne looked down, a bloody tear dropping from her face when Anna's eyes cracked open. Bethany Anne turned. "Okay, Mr. President, your job is to protect this woman."

He turned to look at Bethany Anne, her eyes glowing red and pulsating red veins webbing her face. Her voice, dark and dangerous as her eyes focused on the men, spoke loud enough that all in the large ballroom could hear her over the gunfire and shouting.

"You want me?" she asked. "You got me!" As she walked toward the other side of the room, red balls of energy materialized in her outstretched hands. She ducked a couple bullets aimed in her direction. "The Queen Bitch is in the house, motherfuckers!" She threw two red balls of energy that slammed into the front two terrorists. Both bodies crashed backward into the wall, the fronts of their bodies burned, eyes open, pupils gone, and nothing but the whites of their eyes visible.

The terrorists right outside the window started screaming in fear.

John, relieved that Bethany Anne was okay, amped up his speed when he heard the screams of the men behind him.

John's smile turned maniacal when he felt the beginning of her fear reach the lobby. John added his own, and now the terrorists knew *real* terror.

John laughed. "You guys let loose the djinn tonight!" He turned his righthand pistol up to ten, then his left. "Let's see how well your bodies stop a Dukes on ten, you naked cock-ball-wanking fuckwits!"

Bodies started exploding, and John's hands started hurting.

Fuck it, they would heal.

ArchAngel stated, "Captain Jameson, fourteen locations identified from the SAM missiles fired."

Captain Paul Jameson was standing in for Gabrielle, who was back on the QBBS *Meredith Reynolds.* "Do we have any Nightshades down yet?"

"Twelve seconds until deployment for locations one through seven on the screen. Two other Nightshade deployments will be on target within seventeen seconds for the rest."

Paul chewed on his cheek, thinking about whether to hit the first group ASAP. That could give the second targets an extra five seconds to react. If he waited until all were targeted before release, that was five extra seconds to send up additional SAMs.

SAMs that seemed particularly effective. How they were tracking them he hadn't figured out quite yet.

"Wait three seconds and deploy first group, then deploy second and third Nightshades as soon as possible."

"Understood, Captain Jameson."

Anna, struggling against the fear, was holding onto the ex-President's arm like a lifeline. He had put the gun to the side and was doing his best to just stay with Anna, holding onto her and fighting to not run away. He had to yell at more than one person who might have stumbled across Anna already. He had no idea how Bethany Anne's blood had helped the woman heal, but it had.

He was still in shock about David. His security guy had cold-bloodedly shot Bethany Anne in the back right in front of him. He hadn't reacted. He would have liked to have thought it was because he didn't see it.

No, he saw it happen, but he had been locked in shock even when Anna had jumped David to stop him from shooting Bethany Anne again. It was when Bethany Anne reached into David's chest and crushed his heart that he started moving again.

Then, Bethany Anne had crumpled when Anna had looked dead... Hell, probably *was* dead.

The first few shots in their direction had prompted him to pick up David's pistol, find the extra magazine he had on him, and start firing back. All the times the Secret Service had given him rudimentary instruction had helped.

A few seconds ago he had been sure that they were all going to die, but now he wasn't sure any terrorists were going to survive the night.

What had they unleashed?

Bethany Anne grabbed the man who was desperately trying to crawl out the window and pulled him back, screaming. Her punch caved in the side of his head. She jumped to the windowsill and then off the sill, landing ten feet below on the grass.

She picked up a Kalashnikov and started cracking off shots at those running from her. As she walked forward, she fired until she ran out of bullets, then grabbed a fresh magazine and continued shooting. She heard John laughing behind her and to her right, so she dropped the rifle and ran that way.

Ayaan had been trying to open the latest box when they were hit, and the other four on the roof of the building were celebrating when the whistling started. Ayaan had looked up and was seeking to identify the noise when Ahmed beside him exploded into red mist.

The men started calling out to the Holy One, but their cries couldn't be heard.

The other three exploded one by one, the whistling loud enough to hurt Ayaan's ears as he lay flat on the roof praying to the Prophet for his life.

The noise left as quickly as it arrived and Ayaan looked around at the gore and body parts strewn over the rooftop. He crawled to the side of the building, leaned his head over the side, and threw up.

John could feel Bethany Anne as she came up from his left. He had precious few targets left. Well, live targets.

There were some who were wounded. Perhaps they might be

saved, but all John cared was they were out of commission and not a threat.

It was up to others whether they lived or not.

Because they had to wait until the missiles after them were spent, the five Black Eagles arrived too late to get involved in the firefight. Black Eagle One landed in the courtyard in a space without too many body parts.

Rishaan jumped out of the Black Eagle and palmed it closed, and it rose a hundred feet in the air. It was the easiest way to keep nosy people from trying to get into it, yet keep it almost immediately available for use.

He walked over to the door and met John coming from the other direction.

John holstered his left pistol to shake hands with the pilot. "Rishaan, good to see you. What happened?"

"SAMs, John," he told the Queen's Bitch. "I don't know where they got the technology, but they were able to track us for a little while. We stayed close enough to them so they didn't return."

"I was wondering why you didn't just outrun them," John observed.

"ArchAngel wasn't sure if they had the logic to come back and hit you here, so we stayed out there as bait until their engines spent their fuel."

"Away from land?"

Rishaan nodded. "Yeah. If they hit a boat... Well, we tried our best to minimize the casualties."

John looked around the courtyard. "I'm sure we will get the blame for the deaths, instead of these poor misunderstood bastards."

Rishaan looked around at the carnage. "Shaytan's dogs, all of them."

John turned to the hotel to check on Bethany Anne and Anna. This night could only get worse, not better.

"Rishaan," he called.

"Yes?"

"Get back in your ship and stay close. I might need to call down a few attitude adjustments." John walked into the hotel. He was covered in blood and guts, and needed a shower badly.

"My luck someone got this shit on video."

Something he didn't want to think about crunched under his shoe.

CHAPTER SEVENTEEN

QBBS *Meredith Reynolds*

The *Meredith Reynolds'* Defensive EI Reynolds' male voice came over the speakers. "General, we have unexpected incoming."

Lance looked up from his desk in main Defense Operations. To date it had been a very sophisticated office for Lance, Dan, Kevin, and a few others to use. They expected to be busy once they went through the annex gate, but not here in their own solar system. He looked at Dan, who shrugged and got up from his desk to join Lance.

"What do we have, Reynolds?" Lance asked.

"Sporadic and faint positive hits one hundred twelve kilometers off Area 312 outside the docks, sir." A hologram appeared, showing the QBBS *Meredith Reynolds* with the docks highlighted in orange and a faint blue light flickering off to the side.

"Velocity?" Dan asked.

"Matching with us at the moment," Reynolds answered. "It was slowly approaching until three minutes ago."

"Was that why the ten- and five-thousand-kilometer warnings didn't go off?" Dan asked.

"Yes, at that point the speed and radar signature determined a minimal threat assessment," the EI replied.

"Huh, something for the after-action report," Lance commented. "Reynolds, backtrack likely origination point."

"Five days ago, Earth orbit."

"And there is *another* item for the AAR," Dan inserted. He looked at Lance. "Country or our unfriendly UFO group?"

"I'm going with unfriendly UFO group for five hundred," Lance answered as he rubbed his chin, "but is this a kamikaze, an attack, or spying?"

"At the rate we're heading toward the gate, everyone on Earth must know we're going to meet up there and probably leave within the month, right?" Dan muttered, but he didn't expect an answer.

ADAM, however, came over the speakers. "Dan, the generally held consensus is that the Etheric Empire will stay at the annex gate for an unspecified amount of time."

"You know, ADAM, you're better than the morning paper," Lance told him.

"Thank you, General."

"So why is he staying out there?" Dan asked. "You think we should send out a greeting party?"

"Well—" Lance started before ADAM interrupted.

"*ATTACK!* Bethany Anne is under attack at the event in Belgium."

"Well, shit!" Lance spat. "There's our answer."

"Reynolds!"

"Sir?"

"Put up the gravitic shield and set it to four kilometers, focused around the docks."

"Meredith!"

"General?" the feminine voice replied.

"Issue the emergency warnings. Shut down the mag-trains and lower the blast doors between the docks and In-World."

"Yes, sir," she replied, and cut her connection.

"Well, their ship just lit up." Dan pointed at the hologram. "Here it comes."

"Reynolds, calculate the lag between when the attack on Bethany Anne started and when that ship reacted," Lance told the EI.

"Could be on a pre-planned time schedule," Dan advised.

Lance insisted, "Yeah, but I'd still like to know." The two men watched as the dot rapidly approached. "I wonder what the hell they think they're going to accomplish?"

MJ-12 Ship XJ-03

Antony Rikert, main pilot on this trip for Majestic 12, spoke over the internal comm system. "Hey, hope our packages are ready down there. We are less than forty-five seconds from ejection."

Tyler came back, "We're good here, one to go. How we looking up there?"

Antony looked over his dash. "So far nothing seems to be coming after us, so that's a good thing."

"That fucker is huge, Tony," Tyler shot back. "They might think we're going to smash on the side or something."

"Possibly, but check this out. For some insane reason they have a large glass viewing area where a bunch of docks are. I'm thinking we shoot our packages over there. They can sacrifice a couple of guys taking out the glass instead of trying against the massive metal doors, and once the air has escaped we go in that way with the additional sacrificial warriors."

"I'll tell them the plan down here," Tyler replied.

"Works for me. Antony out."

John Abdullah Khizen nodded to the man locking his helmet on, then turned with care in his spacesuit, shuffled across the deck, and with help, laid down in the ejection module. They looked like metal caskets to him.

Perhaps that was appropriate.

Inside he could see the explosive packages. The Majestic people had held a demonstration a day ago and everyone in his group agreed the destruction was very impressive and superior to anything they could have brought along.

Further, the men explained, the bombs would not activate until the ejection modules were over six kilometers away from the ship. They wanted no chance a blast wave would affect them.

Which meant they would be ejected eight kilometers away from their target, and immediately upon ejection the modules would fire jets to slow down.

"What happens if the jets fail to fire?" John Abdullah had asked the man helping them get into the modules.

"You explode when the modules hit the space station," Tyler had replied. "It will be a very big boom, we assure you."

John Abdullah just nodded. So long as he wouldn't float in the middle of nowhere until he died from starvation while stuck in a small dark claustrophobic space he would be fine.

He wasn't scared to die, but dying slowly in the dark was a different matter. John Abdullah wouldn't have signed up for that type of operation.

Still, if one was going to die for one's beliefs, being one of the first to die while striking infidels in outer space was something he would be able to say he had done with his life. Or actually, others would.

Tyler made sure John Abdullah was tucked in correctly with nothing to stop a proper seal. He closed the top of the module and locked it down, knocking twice on the top to let the man inside know it was done.

They were on a one-way ticket to meet their god. Perhaps

they wouldn't see light again, but perhaps they would. Tyler didn't expect any of them to live past the next four hours. If they failed to kill themselves, the poison they were breathing along with their oxygen would finish the job.

No one was going to stick around for any inconvenient conversations with TQB if Majestic 12 had anything to say about it.

QBBS *Meredith Reynolds*

An alarm went off in the docks, and Meredith's voice reverberated throughout the space. "This is not a drill! This is not a drill! Reynolds is tracking enemy incoming. Repeat, Reynolds is tracking enemy incoming. Please move to designated safety areas. Mag-tram is shut down and In-World is no longer accessible."

Bobcat looked out the viewing glass from his place at the high-top table. He, William, and Marcus had been by themselves having a little celebratory dinner and drinks when Meredith's 'all-areas' warning reverberated throughout the docks.

Marcus turned around in his seat to look out the large viewing window. "I bet you each a quarter-ounce of gold they try to come in through here."

William got up from his chair and walked over to the window, then turned to Marcus, who was still seated. "Here?" he asked, pointing at the glass.

Marcus nodded yes.

William shrugged and turned back to look at outer space. "Okay, I'm in for a quarter-ounce."

Bobcat slid off his barstool chair and knocked on their table. "I'm in." He joined William at the glass.

Marcus' shoulders slumped. He lifted the napkin from his lap and cleaned his mouth before folding it and putting it beside his plate on the table, then slid out of his chair and stood next to Bobcat.

Bobcat turned to look at him. "Why are you thinking they'll hit here?"

William snorted from the other side. "Has to be most likely location. All the other entrances are closed with metal."

"If it was so obvious," Bobcat turned toward William, "why did you bet?"

"I'm supporting Marcus' slide into the terrible vice of gambling. He doesn't do it enough."

"So...what? You're thinking if he wins he might do it more often?" Bobcat asked, and William nodded. Bobcat thought about his answer and turned to look out the window. "I completely support the financial sacrifice on your part, William. Do you mind me taking his side?"

"Sorry, bets are already closed," William told him.

"Damn, just my luck." Bobcat looked at Marcus. "Was that your reason for betting?"

Marcus chuckled, "No. My reason was that *I'm* here, so with my luck they are going to attack where I am." He paused, then added, "If I'm right and die, I don't have to pay off anyway. Kind of a 'win but can't really lose' situation."

"You, Marcus," William stated, "are sneaky. I'm impressed."

Marcus leaned back to look around Bobcat at William. "Enough to go for a full ounce?"

William barked a laugh. "Hell, no! You've already explained your logic. That wasn't smart, young Padawan gambler."

"Oh." Marcus turned back to the window. "Yeah, that wasn't smart of me. I'll do better next time, Master William."

"It is not whether you bet." William's voice sounded old and high-pitched, "but how often you win that matters."

Bobcat called, "Meredith?"

"Yes, Bobcat?"

"Reynolds has the All Guns Blazing defensive measures on, right?"

"Yes, Bobcat."

"Good." Bobcat returned to looking out the window. "This is going to be a good view, guys." He looked around. "I want a fresh beer. Wonder if we have time?"

"You have a minimum of fifty-two seconds, Bobcat," Meredith informed him.

Bobcat's face lit up, "Shit, I'm going for it!" He took off to the closest stairs and the two guys heard his stomping as he raced down. His voice called back, "Hold my spot!"

The two men turned to each other after watching Bobcat's headlong race off the viewing deck.

"I'll go double or nothing that he doesn't make it back up here in time," William offered.

Marcus shook his head. "No bet."

"Damn."

Lance checked the information about Bethany Anne coming in from ArchAngel. The ambush on her had been well planned. They had done a good job, and prepared for her calling in backups.

"They had no idea who they were really hitting," Dan commented. Lance turned to look at him. Dan nodded to the screen that Lance was viewing. "These people don't know about the UnknownWorld. If they did, they wouldn't have hit her with lots of people and regular weapons. They would have tried a small tactical nuke or something similar."

Lance turned back to the report screens. "If you're trying to help me feel better, you suck at it."

Dan smiled. "She's going to be fine." Then he sighed. "The world? I'm not so sure."

"Why?" Lance asked.

"Because I see here," Dan stepped up and pointed at some notes, "that Anna was hurt. Knowing Bethany Anne, she went full 'Queen Bitch' on them."

There was a moment of silence before Lance nodded. "Right in front of everybody."

"Yup. Probably not putting that genie back in the bottle."

Lance shrugged. "She was cracking under the pressure of staying nice all the time anyway, Dan."

"You think so?"

Lance nodded.

"Why? I haven't noticed anything," Dan asked.

"She was withdrawing a little more each week, every time she had to turn the other cheek, to stay nice or tell her people to stay nice," Lance informed him.

Dan took a deep breath and let it out slowly. "Yeah, I'm kinda done with that bullshit myself." He stepped to another console. "How are we doing with the New Mexico thing?"

"One second, I have an update on our inbound." He and Dan watched the hologram. "What are they sending our way?"

"Looks like metal caskets," Dan replied.

"That's what they will be," Lance agreed. The men got a good look at the ship. "It's our beloved UFO friends again." Lance sounded disgusted. "Reynolds!"

"Sir?"

"Hole those sonsabitches with a one-pound puck. If they run, hit them with J-Interceptors at fifteen-k distance. If they don't leave, scramble two Black Eagles and take them out."

"You don't want to capture them?" Dan asked.

Lance grunted. "They just tried to kill my little girl, Dan."

Dan turned back to the hologram. "Fuck them up, Dad."

"J-Intercepts aren't going to leave two pieces big enough to scratch together to get a spark." The General stared at the hologram.

Dan asked, "What are we going to do about the incoming?"

"Reynolds?" Lance called.

"Yes?"

"Destroy the first fifteen and then let the rest through as close as one hundred meters to where they were going before you stop them."

MJ-12 Ship XJ-03

"That's correct, Base," Antony stated, "The packages are leaving the ship and we are about to head back. This part of the operation has gone well."

Antony listened for a second. "Understood. XJ-03 out."

Antony felt one of the last ejection modules leave the ship, and seconds later he felt the last leave. Tyler called him on the comm.

"All gone, boss. We going to stay or skedaddle?"

"We are already," Antony responded, typing in the final coordinates and stabbing the execute button, "leaving."

The large asteroid was getting smaller when the ship's puncture alarm started blaring. Antony swore viciously and sealed his suit. "Tyler, what the hell happened?"

Antony shoved the speed into the red, ignoring additional alarms as the craft shot away from the asteroid.

"Tyler!" Antony called again, but got nothing. The alarms were now muffled, since loss of atmosphere meant the sound couldn't carry. Antony unbelted from his chair and raced to the stairs that led below.

Jumping down them three at a time, he dropped to the lower deck and ran halfway around the circular hallway to reach the part of the ship where Tyler had been working. Antony peered through the glass into the room, then he slammed the wall next to the door.

"Dammit!" Antony turned and slid down the wall, his heart

breaking at the sight of his friend's mangled flesh and blood splattered all over the walls inside the room.

Antony never even heard the microsecond warning before two objects slammed through his craft.

QBBS *Meredith Reynolds*

William and Marcus could hear Bobcat's footsteps as he came back up the stairs with bottles clinking in his hands.

"Did I miss anything?" he asked his friends as he passed William a cold beer and Marcus a Coke. It was a condition of Bethany Anne's that they couldn't serve Pepsi in All Guns Blazing.

Pepsi had become a black-market product.

"You have five seconds before contact by objects, which..."

"Ooooohhhhh!" The three men gaped when massive explosions lit up space some distance away.

"Pretty fireworks, but too far away to know where they were going," William told the other two.

"Five objects have been permitted to come closer," Meredith reported.

Within seconds, the men saw reflections from the five metal objects heading toward the glass viewing deck.

Bobcat took a swig of his beer, then used the bottle to point out the window. "Motherfuckers, didn't you think we considered this?" he asked no one in particular.

"Fuck me," Disgust colored William's voice. "I'm out a quarter-ounce of gold."

Dulce Lake, New Mexico, USA

Patrick slammed his office phone down and spat, "Son of a *bitch!*" He jumped up, grabbed a chair, and threw it ten feet to slam against a rock wall. "*FUCK!*" he screamed.

He had just received word they lost communications with XJ-03.

Patrick looked around and could only see red. He wanted to beat the shit out of anything and everything.

"FUCK!" he screamed once more. He walked back and put his hands on his desk, his head hanging down as he squeezed his eyes shut. He tried not to think about his last talk with Antony and Tyler before they left.

"How did they find them?" he whispered into his empty office.

"How?"

QBBS *Meredith Reynolds*

"All I'm saying," Marcus insisted. "Is this is the stupidest idea we've come up with yet."

"Oh, shut up and turn around. It's going to get us drinks for decades." Bobcat laughed as he turned away from the window and reached for his belt.

Outside QBBS *Meredith Reynolds*

John Abdullah's module started beeping, and red lights lit inside. Apparently something had stopped them from making it all the way to the asteroid, but the small air jets would be able to get them close enough. The lid opened on his module.

He used his feet to help him pull up, and he looked around. He was amazed at the clarity of view space offered. He had a very tiny rotation, so he reached over and hit the two buttons that would stop it.

He moved slowly, as they had been taught. Fast movement was not your friend in space.

When he was able to bring his head around to see the asteroid more fully, his eyes opened wide at the sight in front of him.

. . .

QBBS *Meredith Reynolds*

"What are those three up to now?" Dan asked.

"What three?" Lance asked as he issued commands to those who had been secreted in New Mexico and read reports on Bethany Anne's situation.

"Team BMW, who else?" Dan answered. "Oh, *hell* no!" He burst out laughing. "Holy shit, Lance, you have *got* to see this!"

Outside QBBS *Meredith Reynolds*

John Abdullah was puzzled by what exactly he was seeing, but he finally had to admit it was exactly what he had thought it was originally.

There were one black and two white asses pressed against glass, aimed at him.

QBBS *Meredith Reynolds*

"Hahahahahaha!" Bobcat, William, and Marcus were all trying to catch their breath.

"Lord, I would *love* to know what those sumbitches are thinking right now." William wiggled his butt across the glass. "Need a moon to figure out where you are, you fucking duck spunk?" he called over his shoulder toward those outside the huge window.

Marcus gasped. "Einstein, forgive me now, but this is fucking funny!"

"That's it!" Bobcat called, taking a swig of his beer. "Pull on that chain, motherfuckers, and win a one way trip to Hell… It's the one with two orbs on top!"

The men, laughing their asses off, hadn't heard the footsteps coming up the stairs.

"What the hell are you three doing?" A woman's voice cut through their laughter.

All three men, still bent over with their naked asses pushed up against the window, looked over to their left. Gabrielle, her mouth agape, stood there staring at them.

They were grinning like little boys.

"Mooning those assholes!" Bobcat answered, jerking a thumb over his shoulder.

Gabrielle took a few steps onto the deck and peeked around to see the last handful of men trying to get out of their ejection modules.

"Are those terrorists?" she asked, confused. She looked at the three men, pants around their feet on the floor, and then at the obviously lousy space-walking terrorists outside.

'Yeah, we think so," William agreed. "Meredith said the first fifteen explosions were high-level sophisticated devices that didn't need oxygen."

"So you three are mooning terrorists?" she asked, seeking confirmation.

"Uh, yeah, pretty much." Bobcat was still grinning like a kid while he took a swig of his beer.

"Oh," she replied.

Outside QBBS _Meredith Reynolds_

John Abdullah's face wrinkled in further annoyance when another white butt was pressed against the window and aimed at him and his brothers.

Those playing with them at the moment wouldn't laugh when they got close enough to explode their bombs!

QBBS _Meredith Reynolds_

The defensive operations room had filled with people. There

were screens all over the room, but the large main screen in the middle wasn't focused on the enemy.

Meredith had scrambled three small working cams that had been used for outside maintenance in the last six months. Now the EI was using them to take video from behind the terrorists, who had no idea the little units were there. The cameras were pointed at All Guns Blazing.

"Meredith," Dan called.

"Yes?"

"Zoom back in on the window," he told her, trying to figure out what the hell… "Oh, Lord!" Dan cracked up and the others started laughing too.

"Kiss it, you fucking posers!" Gabrielle yelled. "Hey, pass that beer over here!"

Bobcat reached over and grabbed William's beer.

"Hey!" he objected.

Bobcat passed it to Marcus, who passed it to Gabrielle. "Gabrielle knows better than to ask for mine!" Bobcat told his friend, who shrugged as they continued their mirth.

"I wonder if she knows her ass is being taped for posterity?" Lance asked Dan.

"Well… Now, whose fucking ass is that?" Dan asked when a fifth object pressed against the glass.

"Go!" Bobcat yelled as the black German Shepherd turned around and pushed her rear against the window.

She chuffed.

"Hell yeah! That's right!" Gabrielle laughed as Ashur's mate chuffed additional comments about the men outside.

"This is getting *Gott Verdammt* ridiculous." Lance was trying not to laugh his ass off. "Oh, Lord Almighty. Well, five asses for five assholes. I think we have enough for now. Reynolds!"

"Sir?"

"Tell those clowns to zip up. We're getting rid of the trash..."

Reynolds' voice came out of the speakers in the viewing area. "Gentlemen, Lady, and Bellatrix, General Reynolds requested that you be informed to zip up and watch."

"Oh good!" Marcus reached down for his pants. "Who the hell is going to clean the glass?"

The five of them turned and the four humans put their clothes back in the right places.

The five men outside started struggling frantically as the gravitic shield pushed them slowly away from the docks, then sped up to push the men just short of when they would likely pass out.

"Now that," Marcus commented, "is terminal velocity."

Out in space, John Abdullah could only scream in the darkness.

CHAPTER EIGHTEEN

The sirens got closer as Bethany Anne walked into the ballroom. The smell of burned flesh was still pungent from the two terrorists she had toasted with the balls of energy she had hurled at them.

The men and women in the room stank of fear.

Anna turned to watch as Bethany Anne came toward them. The ex-President held her up, concerned about her health.

When Bethany Anne walked through the doors, people shrank back against the walls. She looked at them as she made her way to the corner where Anna and the ex-President were, feet away from David's dead body.

"What are you?" one of the women hissed at Bethany Anne.

"A mad-as-hell recently-shot-in-the back pissed-off bitch who is going to stick her foot up your butt if you don't learn how to be polite to someone who just saved your scrawny useless ass," Bethany Anne told her as she continued toward the corner.

Bethany Anne's concern was evident as she knelt. "How are you, Anna?"

"Alive?" Anna Elizabeth responded. "What happened?"

"C'mon," she reached under Anna and easily picked her up in

her arms. She turned toward the entrance and, looking at the ex-President, she asked, "You coming, or are you staying with your man here?"

The ex-President stared at David's body and rolled down his sleeves. "I have no idea what he was up to, Bethany Anne."

"I know now, but I didn't suspect when he shot me. He was mind-tapped by an enemy group who is using some seriously badass mental shit." John Grimes, himself a bloody mess, strode into the room and the stink of fear ratcheted up higher.

What the fuck was it about John? Bethany Anne wondered. *I fucking have glowing red eyes and damn near horns sticking out of my head, but it's John who still causes a shit-ton of fear when they didn't even see him do anything?*

Something to consider some other night.

"John, please take Anna." He nodded and gently took Anna from Bethany Anne.

"Hey, I can walk," Anna argued.

"Shut up, Anna. This is the only time you are going to be touching John like this, or his woman will shoot you a final time herself. Stop trying to be a hero and allow your recently-shot-to-shit-self to be carried, all right?"

Anna nodded and put her head on John's chest.

She was asleep almost immediately.

"So he was manipulated?" the ex-President asked.

"Yes," Bethany Anne confirmed. "He didn't know what was going on. He was a pawn in a bigger game."

"Fuck." The ex-President looked around the room. "I won't leave him here."

"Well, in for a penny, in for a shit-ton of copper." Bethany Anne picked David's body up.

More intake of breath and muttering in other languages occurred when David's body suddenly disappeared into thin air.

"What the hell?" the ex-President exclaimed.

"He's in a foreign dimension. He'll be fine until I pull him back out. We need to go."

>> Bethany Anne, your Executive Pod is waiting outside.<<

"Okay guys, ride's here. Let's go." She had started walking toward the exit when one of the men called from the other corner that she couldn't just leave.

Bethany Anne flipped him off. "Stop us, bitch!"

They had almost made it to the front of the hotel when she called over her shoulder, "The Directorate of Special Units and other people are congregating outside. Stay here until I explain the situation to them."

The two men halted as Bethany Anne continued walking toward the front doors.

"How will she explain all this..." the ex-President looked around, "death and destruction?" He turned toward John. "And can she really get David's body back? I'm not sure what the hell is real anymore."

"Yes to your second question—she can get him back. As to the first, I imagine she isn't so much going to explain what happened as explain what *will* happen," John answered.

"What's going to happen?" the ex-President asked, half-listening.

"She's going to tell anyone outside we're leaving," John replied.

"They aren't going to want to hear that," he cautioned.

"She doesn't give a shit what they want at the moment."

Three different FN SCARS were pulled up to shoulders and aimed at her as Bethany Anne exited the hotel. Lights had been set up, illuminating the courtyard. She used the moment the cops needed to confirm she wasn't an enemy to check out the carnage John had wrought.

Damn, he'd been busy out here. She made a face and stepped over a particularly large puddle. Her feet almost adhered to the ground from the sticky blood.

Gott Verdammt, this was nasty shit.

"Get on the ground!" a voice using a megaphone called.

Bethany Anne looked up, shock evident on her face. "Are you fucking crazy?"

"I said..." Megaphone Man started again.

"I heard you, you sick fuck!" she retorted. "Does anywhere," she pointed around her, "look like a place you want to stick hands or, God forbid, your face?"

"Who are you?" the voice called back after a moment of reflection.

"I'm the one who needs to put my shoes back on so that when I kick your ass you know it!" she replied as she stepped over another couple of bodies. "Oh, that's just fucking gross." She made a face. "Any of you people who are presently aiming your guns at little ole me going to come lay down your jacket so I don't have to walk on this shit?"

Bethany Anne listened to the heated whispering coming from the vehicles set up behind the lights.

"Sir!" It was a male voice. "That's the TQB CEO."

An older voice replied, "The one up in outer space?"

"Yes."

"What's she doing here?" the person in charge hissed back.

"She," Bethany Anne pointed to herself, interrupting the hastily-whispered conversation, "is trying to warn you that you need to move your asses or you're going to have a very bad hair day in about half a minute."

"Why?" the person in charge called back.

"Because thirty seconds is the maximum amount of patience I have left!" she explained. "If I wasn't trying to not flush the good cops down the toilet with these," she pointed around her, "terrorist assholes, I'd already have..." Bethany Anne flashed sideways, using her Etheric-enhanced speed to pivot, run outside of the lights and up the side of the courtyard behind the cops. She stopped right behind the man with the megaphone. She hissed into his ear, "kicked your ass!"

There was shock written on his face.

"Yes, I'm leaving of my own free will," the ex-President told the lead police officer a fourth time, "and if you don't get out of my way, my ride is going to leave without me."

Frustrated, but not seeing how the previous president of the United States could be under the mind control of the accused mutant or demon-possessed CEO of TQB, he nodded his head and waved to his men to let the ex-President join the TQB people already in their Pod. The ex-President walked over and stepped into the Pod, and within seconds it disappeared into the night sky.

The cop looked around. How the hell was he going to explain this?

Bethany Anne handed the ex-President some wipes. "Have anything you need to clean?" He looked at her and did a doubletake.

She was clean and had fresh clothes on.

He turned around and saw John in the seat behind them, but Anna was missing. "What happened? Is Anna in the same place as David's body?" He turned back to Bethany Anne. "Is Anna alive?"

"Yes," she answered. "Anna is alive and fine. I took her up to *ArchAngel* for further treatment. I took a fast shower and changed clothes because...ugh." She looked out the window for a second.

"Sticky bloody clothes are the worst." She turned back to him. "So...questions?"

The moment drew out. He seemed to be weighing which question to ask first before finally squaring his shoulders. "Did you know David was under mind control when you killed him?"

She returned his stare. "No, not until the pain of his death released it." Her shoulders slumped. "Perhaps if I had paused to consider he was acting out of character I might have been able to figure it out, but—"

"But," John interrupted from behind her, "Bethany Anne has a catastrophically bad reaction when she's shot in the back."

Bethany Anne turned to say something to John, but he put up a hand. "It all goes back to Petre, Bethany Anne. No one can survive an experience like that and not be changed. If you get shot or hurt somehow from behind you immediately go into a protective mode, which usually means you immediately attempt to remove the threat."

"You've been shot in the back before?" the ex-President asked. "I feel like I've fallen into the Twilight Zone."

John started counting on his fingers. "She's been shot, stabbed, burned, shot some more, cut with swords, and also with other sharp instruments including claws and fangs." He paused a second.

"Not helping, John." Bethany Anne told him.

The ex-President asked, "Why didn't David's bullet's blow you away? I just noticed a couple of shoulder wounds."

"Bethany Anne doesn't go anywhere without back protection now. She's wearing a specially designed flexible metal shield that's about an eighth of an inch thick," John supplied.

"How did you keep it on?" he asked, curious how this woman kept protection on her when he would have sworn she didn't have a vest on underneath that white blouse.

"Sticky glue," she answered. "The protection goes on in sections so I can move around easily. If I need to look presentable once the sections are on, a skin-colored cover is placed on my back as well."

"Oh," he replied.

"No, there isn't anything up front," she told him. "I worry about my back getting shot. If someone's in front of me, I can deal with that."

John leaned toward the ex-President and whispered, "And she hates how the protection hurts the precious pair."

"John Grimes!" Bethany Anne's voice was half-embarrassed, half-exasperated. "This is the ex-President of the United-fuck-ing-States!" She pointed a finger at him. "You have been around Tabitha way too damned much."

"I haven't seen Tabitha in weeks," he protested.

"Which obviously was still too recently." She dropped her finger and addressed the ex-President. "We're going to be at your house in a few minutes. This gets you there before anyone can react to the situation, so you can decide what you want to do."

The rest of the trip was silent, with everyone in quiet contemplation until Bethany Anne received a call from her father.

Two men stepped out of the black Audi A-6 with license plate A-216, and the lead officer walked over. One of the gentlemen looked at the carnage. "I'll be back."

Finn Jacobs closed his door and waited for the special directorate contact who was headed in his direction.

Those that knew license plates numbers knew he was from the government.

Finn held out his hand. "Eden, right?"

The officer nodded. "Yes. Good to meet you, Mr. Jacobs."

"Call me Finn." He glanced around. "Looks like we have a huge mess here."

Eden gazed at the carnage as well. "We do. We also have ten

rooftops with more bodies, and we suspect at least a couple of more."

"Rooftops?" Finn asked.

"Yes. The terrorists used shoulder-mounted SAMs to target the TQB ships."

"I didn't hear about that." Finn rubbed his face. "Sorry, too early in the morning and no coffee yet."

"You really don't want to eat anything right now, sir," Eden advised.

"Who did we lose inside?"

"Predominantly guards, two innocent hotel attendees, and at least four of the hotel employees."

"How about the special guests inside?"

"You knew about this meeting?" Eden asked.

"Not until I woke up this morning," Finn replied. "I got an update from my partner, who's out looking around."

"Someone I should know about?" Eden asked.

Finn shrugged. "It could become a problem to know more about him, but I'll leave that in your hands to decide."

Eden shrugged it off. If he needed to know, he'd ask him. He nodded toward the hotel. "So far none of the VIPs inside except one are dead. That death was VIP-on-VIP violence."

Finn's eyebrow raised.

"Seems, for whatever reason, the ex-President of the United States' security put three or four rounds into the back of TQB's CEO. The negotiator for TQB jumps him, he puts two rounds into her and she drops to the ground, then TQB's CEO becomes some sort of demon and punches through his chest and kills him. She forces blood into her negotiator's mouth and terrorists start shooting as they come in through a broken window. Her security is busy shooting the shit out of… well," he pointed to the dead in the courtyard, "all these shit-heads. The ex-President takes over guarding the negotiator, who is apparently reviving, and our demon CEO starts walking toward the terrorists trying to get in through the window."

"Did you say three or four rounds in the back?" Finn asked. "I'm just trying to figure out how she stood up."

"The injury we could see was in her shoulder, so the thinking is she had some sort of super-high-tech bulletproof vest or something on under her clothes."

"She bleeds?" Finn asked.

Eden looked at him and spoke slowly. "Yes, and apparently it makes her angry."

"I think I would be fuck-all angry if someone shot me in the back, especially if they were supposed to be protecting me."

"Not *this* kind of angry," Eden told him.

"Okay, surprise me. What kind of angry?"

"The brilliant red eyes-kind that creates glowing red balls of energy she throws into two of the terrorists, energy balls that somehow burn the shit out of them. Killed them and burned their eyes completely white."

"Okay, I'm surprised." Finn thought about it. "What kind of technology does she have that she can create red balls of energy, and where did the energy come from?" he wondered. "So they took the body of the guy she killed, right?" Finn asked, "I mean, we didn't get lucky and she left us that guy?"

"Uh, well, the guy is gone," Eden equivocated, "but no, they didn't take the body with them. Eyewitnesses inside say she did something and the body just disappeared."

Finn looked up into the night. This project was getting more and more frustrating. Finally he looked back at Eden. "Video?"

"Well, that's where we got lucky," Eden answered.

Tanya hid in the shadows a mile from the ambush that had gone so terribly wrong.

What the hell *was* that woman?

Her feed from the hotel video had allowed her to see the beautiful opening salvo in the operation. The freedom fighters had done an amazing job of surprising the gate guards. No hesitation to kill, just focused on getting inside, and it looked like the extra fighters Abdullah had brought to this little party in TQB's honor was going to be a wise move.

It was supposed to be Bethany Anne's final going-away present from Majestic 12. Apparently Tanya's attempts to learn about Bethany Anne's security had missed a few very important things.

Such as being fucking bulletproof and throwing around balls of burning energy like some sort of comic-book hero.

Tanya successfully resisted the desire to throw her phone.

She was in the basement of an old empty hotel. She was chewing on the inside of her cheek and deciding what she needed to do next when she got a call on her private line.

One from the home office, so to speak.

She picked up the phone and put it to her ear. "Yes?" She listened to Patrick's monotone recitation of events in space. Her shoulders drooped, her eyes closed, and she replied, "I got it. We lost Antony and Tyler. No, the mission here was a bust. I'm sending you an InfoBurst in a few minutes, then I've got to get out of here. I don't want to be caught in a dragnet. What? No. No, let me find my own way back to base. I need some time to process everything."

Tanya grabbed the little wireless mouse she was using for her computer and started flipping it end over end as she listened to Patrick talk.

"No, I don't know what happened to any of the men here. Yes, I implanted the dead man's signal in Abdullah per our operations and tactics rules. Me, you, I don't care. Here, hold on."

Tanya stopped flipping her mouse and set it back on the little pad. Clicking on a text box, she typed in a code and clicked 'Send.'"

She went back to her call. "Okay, Abdullah, if he was alive, is now brain-dead. He was the last complication from the operation here."

"Yeah, I'll miss them too. Yeah, we *will* fuck them up, that's for damn sure." She listened for another few moments. "Okay, I'll be back within seventy-two hours. Bye."

Tanya hung up the phone and put it down. She reached for the little mouse and as the first tear dropped down her face she threw it against the far wall. "*FUUUUCK!*"

She put her head down on the little table that held her laptop, her shoulders heaving as the tears soaked the floor beneath her.

She wasn't sure how long she had been crying when her early warning alarms started beeping. She jerked up, noting the movement alarms in the alley on the south side of the building. "Dammit!"

The wolf, a female, was following a scent she had picked up in the group of the men from earlier. Her love had told her that whenever one tried to figure out the truth, if something didn't belong it was usually the string to pull to get an answer.

Since Stephen was so old, Jennifer gave him the benefit of the doubt as to whether it was true or not. Age was supposed to bring wisdom. He certainly had the age, Jennifer just hoped it equaled wisdom.

Behind her, five men in tactical gear glided through the night. The scent went into a building. She waited for the men to come and open the door for her.

Door opened, she looked around for traps and sniffed to see if she could detect any explosives.

Clean.

She padded into the foyer of the empty building.

Jennifer followed the trail to a door that led down. Being careful, she and the five men opened the door and checked out the landing before slowly descending. One of the men released multiple three-inch drones that checked down the staircase before giving off a beep the five men could hear in their implants.

Two minutes later the team broke into the bottom basement, only to find that no one was inside.

Jennifer changed back to human right next to a wall, disgust evident in her voice. "The bitch went through here somehow." The team tried to figure out how to open the hidden door, but three minutes later they got the call to return to the *ArchAngel*.

Two miles away Tanya came up out of the bolt hole, checking over her shoulder with alarm in her eyes as she remembered the size of the wolf the team chasing her had with them.

Who the hell brings a wolf to find someone?

CHAPTER NINETEEN

The Etheric

Bethany Anne stood with John, who was holding a body bag. Both had their heads down.

"I made a mistake and for that, David Dennison, I am sorry," Bethany Anne told body lying between them. "Perhaps if I had opened my mind I could have figured out something was wrong, but I reacted in pain and frustration. I allowed my anger to be unleashed—"

"Boss, you can't," John interrupted, but stopped when Bethany Anne put up a hand.

"I understand, John," she agreed, "but David needs to know I don't blame him. He was a pawn, between two powerful forces he couldn't understand. Perhaps...just perhaps, I'll figure out a way to slow down enough to find a better solution next time." She stood for a moment, saying a final prayer for another person caught up in the politics of power. She wiped away a tear and nodded.

"John, would you help me with the body?" she asked, and reached for the bag he was holding.

. . .

Dulce Lake Area, New Mexico, USA

Ztopik was waiting for the two humans, curiosity abating his normal desire to play with their emotions. In the history of his time with these two leaders they had never requested an unscheduled meeting.

Something must have substantially affected them.

While annoyed—he was in the middle of reviewing the tests in Section Four with the human-N'thyruuk mutations—this interaction with the humans might bring something new to his existence as he plotted to find the right mutation to compete in the great wars.

Moments later, he received the mental update that the two humans were outside. Ztopik stood up.

He preferred to hold all his discussions from the advantage of height. Humans seemed to defer to those taller than themselves. Perhaps it was similar to reactions in canines? He wasn't sure. He would need to isolate the DNA code for that and study it.

The door opened, allowing Patrick Brown and Dr. Eva Hocks into the room.

They stopped and bowed slightly to Ztopik, who paused and then bowed back.

Patrick spoke first. "We appreciate you interrupting your research to hear us, Ambassador Ztopik."

Even more curious, he thought. Rarely was Overseer Patrick this formal. He nodded so Patrick would continue.

"We have had setbacks, and believe there might be an attempt to locate this base, and if successful, to attack it."

"By whom? The US government?" Ztopik asked.

"No, TQB," Eva blurted.

Ztopik turned toward the human woman. "TQB again? I thought they were a technology challenge, not a warlike group."

"We...ahh...we might have been a little mistaken on that," Patrick answered, licking his lips.

Ztopik's unblinking stare returned to Patrick. "Overseer

Patrick, was this an intellectual mistake, or perhaps inadequate information shared on your part?"

"Patrick!" Eva hissed. "Now is not the time to play word games."

Patrick's mouth pressed together before he spoke. "Ztopik, TQB has superior technology, and our many attempts to acquire their technology have failed."

"How could a group with Earth's technology protect themselves from Majestic 12?" Ztopik asked. "I seek clarity here, if you are asking me to help."

Eva shot Patrick a dark look and provided more information. "Ztopik, their people stopped an ambush that would have killed a normal human. Tanya sent a large group of armed men to strike and not only did they fail, but TQB's people killed a lot of them in the process."

Patrick, feeling Eva's concern, finally broke through his hesitancy. "They found and destroyed XJ-03 in space, and on multiple occasions have tracked our ships, coming closer and closer to locating this base."

Ztopik's long sinewy arm went up and held a hand out to Eva, causing her to stop what she was about to say. "Overseer Patrick, TQB is in outer space?" Patrick nodded. "How long have they had this capability?"

Patrick's eyes closed.

He opened them, realizing that hiding TQB from Ztopik had been a mistake. "Years."

"What was XJ-03 after?" Ztopik asked.

"A battle station. TQB has built a battle station in an asteroid."

"A battle station? They have built something for war?" Ztopik asked.

"Actually, a lot of somethings!" Eva hissed, more concerned about TQB coming to their base than her fear of Ztopik.

Ztopik ignored the woman's outburst.

Patrick agreed, "Yes, it's for war. I have documents which

suggest they are heading for a different solar system to fight another alien race."

"The name?" Ztopik asked.

"Bethany Anne," Patrick answered.

"That does not sound like an alien race," Ztopik responded.

"Yollins," Patrick corrected.

"Yollins?" Ztopik thought for a second. "Yes, I know of the Yollins. Powerful, but not very creative in their martial efforts. They expand their systems by subjugating the local intelligent species as slave labor and returning the raw materials necessary for their own species to expand." He didn't say anything for a few moments, and Patrick and Eva looked at each other.

"I am thinking," he told them, interrupting their attempt at mental communication, "that if your TQB has geared up to fight the Yollins, then they must have found and overcome a Yollin research vessel. Otherwise the Yollins would have left the system and reported that this was a poor choice for subjugation."

Ztopik looked at both humans, spending a moment or two on each. "Unlikely."

Then he looked up at the ceiling as if weighing different possibilities. "Or the Yollins would have been back in force and nothing we have built to date would have been enough against a mass assault."

Ztopik was annoyed. His enjoyment of the research into crossing the easily mutable human DNA with so many different species had made him complacent. He didn't fear anything from this planet, but a concerted effort by a large enough space-going competitor would mean that all his work to date would have been in vain. He hadn't left his world and hidden on this horrible little planet to stay in the background.

The Kurtherians played the great game, and Ztopik wished to prove himself against the masters of DNA manipulation and species-on-species war.

"The Yollins' skill would explain how they built in an asteroid and some of their war capabilities. The problem, I believe, is their ignorance. They need more than a battle station to save this planet from subjugation. With Yollins, you either hide your talents so their research vessel leaves..." he paused a second, "or you create a strong-enough military to cause the Yollins to consider you much too difficult to subjugate."

There was another pause as Ztopik's head swayed back and forth on his thin neck. "Then you continue to build your military and try to stay ahead of them."

Patrick's tablet beeped. "My apologies. I'm expecting a video from Tanya to share." He pulled out his handheld and looked at the private message. "Well, shit."

Ztopik held out his long white arm and Patrick handed the tablet to him. He touched a couple buttons so all could hear the video's audio play a second time. He pointed to the tablet. "Who is this female?"

"That," Patrick told him, "is the CEO of TQB."

Ztopik viewed the video a third time. He stopped before playing it a fourth, because the value of seeking new information was offset by a rather unfamiliar emotion, one he hadn't felt since coming to this world.

Heavy concern.

Secret Meeting, UN Building, New York, USA

Ambassadors Zhou, Emeka, and Franklin waited for a fourth to join them as they sipped coffee in the private room.

All three had used what technology they had to confirm this room was bug-free, and all had left their electronics outside.

Ambassador Zhou started, "While we wait for our fourth party, have you read the eyewitness accounts?"

Ambassador Emeka nodded. "If true, then she is a demon and we must do something to protect Earth from her and her kind."

"Do we believe them, though?" Ambassador Franklin asked. "We have no video to prove any of this."

"What good would video be?" Zhou countered. "It is easy to doctor video, and you end up having to trust the people providing the information as to its veracity. No, we are trusting those who have been under great duress, and the evidence acquired by the police after the event."

"What do we know for sure?" Emeka asked Zhou.

"We know that two terrorists were indeed killed by an unknown weapon of devastating power. It burned their flesh and fried their nervous systems. Either of these two things would have killed those men. Well, and the kinetic punch that slammed their bodies against the wall behind them. That probably would have killed them from internal bleeding."

"What weapon does she possess that can accomplish this?" Franklin murmured to himself, wondering what TQB could have built.

"Unknown." Zhou answered the question anyway. "But more intriguing, she was shot and not killed. She took multiple gunshots to her back, and witnesses suggest they saw at least two wounds in her shoulder."

"She can't be killed?" Emeka scoffed.

Zhou shrugged. "We believe she can be killed, but is that the best solution?" he asked.

"I can't think of a better solution at this moment, Zhou. Why would we leave such a danger to challenge the world's will?"

"Who said we would leave that danger walking free?" Zhou replied. "She obviously has physical skills which we can harness to help mankind learn to survive such physical harm." He looked at the two men. "She professes a desire to help mankind? How about she provides the secrets to eternal youth and physical health she is withholding from us?"

"That is not something she will give us willingly," Emeka warned.

There was a soft knock on the door. Ambassador Zhou got up from his chair and leaned over to Emeka and Franklin and whispered, "Who said we planned on asking her *permission?*"

Zhou opened the door and welcomed in a fourth to the meeting in the early hours of the morning. Once he made sure the hallway was empty, Zhou closed the door.

Emeka's eyes widened in surprise. Franklin looked at him, and both had the same thought.

Why was the Ambassador of the United States joining them?

Outside Chicago, Illinois, USA

"Honey?" The ex-President's wife joined him in his study. Dawn was creeping over the trees, and soon the new day would begin.

But would it?

Who do you trust, those who are like you, or those whose actions match yours?

He turned toward her as she walked around his desk to stand next to his chair. "Yes, sweetheart?"

She reached down and pulled him closer. "I'm thankful you came back to us." A teardrop moistened his forehead, and then her fingers wiped it off. "I can't believe David is dead," she whispered, and he felt her hug tighten.

He rested his head on her chest and looked out the window at the dark trees.

No answer to that, just like the questions going through his head right now.

He hadn't received one call from the White House directly. He had gotten messages, but not one personal connection. He speculated about that as he looked out of the window, thinking about the options as he watched a helicopter pass in the distance once more. He was being watched and they could say what they wanted, but he knew they weren't protecting him from Bethany Anne.

No, they wanted to catch her coming back and jail her. Then they would figure out how to keep her legally.

He didn't bother telling them not to try. This wasn't his operation, and he had been trying for three years to explain that change didn't come about by creating a military state where might makes right, especially not when the one with the most might wasn't you.

He sighed. They had picked up David's body two hours before, and now his Secret Service attachment was itching to have a conversation with TQB. If David shot her, then it was warranted.

It was a no-win situation, and it had happened because he had asked Bethany Anne to try communication one more time. The request originated from the White House, and then there was an ambush. He let that percolate in his mind. At this point he wasn't willing to ignore any possibilities.

"Did he deserve to die?" his wife asked.

He focused and realized she had asked the question more than once. "For his actions, yes," he answered, "but he didn't do it of his own free will. He had been brainwashed by someone. Bethany Anne didn't know that until David had shot her, then he shot Anna Elizabeth when she tried to stop him from shooting Bethany Anne again while she was down."

"Oh no! Did he kill her?"

"Almost. She would have died if not for Bethany Anne. Hell, we all would have died if not for Bethany Anne."

"Don't you mean you all would have died because of her?" she asked.

"What, because they attacked us because she was there?" he replied.

"Yes."

"Honey, I was the one who talked her into attending. Are you suggesting I killed David?"

"No!" He felt her clench her hand into a fist and tap it on his shoulder. "Dammit, stop being so civil!"

"You want this to be her fault, but why?" he asked.

"Because I can't change the government!" she exclaimed. "I've been in those halls. I've been around those people. If this isn't her fault, then whose is it?"

His eyebrows drew together and he realized he was ignoring the smaller picture. There comes a time in every man's life when the clarity of the situation becomes stark and unyielding.

This wasn't about the world or the United States or the people in the United States. He had given eight years of his life to make his country the best he could. He had spent another three years trying to mitigate the friction between the present administration and TQB, but now he needed to protect his family and be on the right side of this conflict. A war between the government and TQB.

Unfortunately, he wasn't going to be allowed to sit out this fight. He looked up at his wife. "You know I love you, right?"

She smiled down at him and touched his face. "You've got that look in your eyes." She searched, seeking insight into what he was thinking. "I'm not going to be happy with this, am I?"

"I'll accept my punishment as I have to." The ex-President stood up. "Wake the girls. I've got a call to make."

CHAPTER TWENTY

**ArchAngel,** Orbiting outside L2

The room held fifty humans and six Yollins.

General Lance Reynolds looked at his people and nodded to Dan. "You guys ready for this?"

Dan smiled. "Lance, can't wait to get back into the field again."

"Shit!" Peter called out from the first row. "You know Bethany Anne's coming, right?" There was laughter.

Kiel leaned forward from his position behind Peter and tapped him on the shoulder. Trying to be quiet but failing miserably, he asked Peter in his clicks and twirls before the translation kicked in, "Why is the fact that Bethany Anne is participating something to laugh at?" The Yollin looked around and realized everyone was listening to him. He articulated his shoulders in the gesture he had picked up by watching the humans over the last three years. "I'm sorry, but I am curious."

"I think I understand your confusion, Kiel," Lance answered. "Captain Kael-ven T'chmon and Dan here are going to be in the back, commanding through your people and directing communications and tactics as we clear out the base. You're wondering why it matters that Bethany Anne would be in the back?"

Kiel turned toward him. "Yes, General Reynolds, that is the core of my question."

"Oh," Peter replied, finally understanding the Yollin's question. "I'm sorry, Kiel. I forgot that you and your people haven't been on an operation with Bethany Anne and the Bitches yet."

"Yeah, sometime I'll have to give you the play by play of the Downtown operation after the Everglades operation," Dan interjected. "You'd have a better understanding with that information."

"Or the Chinese base operation," another voice called from behind Kiel. The alien turned to see who had spoken.

Dan's voice caused Kiel to turn back around. "Or the ambush by David that time in the mountains."

"What they are all saying without really telling you, Kiel," Lance broke into those flinging out battle stories, "is that Bethany Anne will be on the tip of the spear, as we call it. She won't be in the back."

"That is the place for those of us who are trained," Kiel answered.

Lance didn't take it as condemnation so much as ignorance. "Kiel, how long have you studied the martial arts? Since how old?"

"Since I was young. When I first left my parents' home I went straight into the military."

"Right. You know I'm Bethany Anne's father, right?" Lance wanted to make sure Kiel understood.

"Yes."

"Bethany Anne has been training to fight since she went into school. She was going to competitive fights and kicking ass when other girls were starting to figure out they liked boys. She has been a warrior in training for almost her whole life. You can't tell her not to be in the front. There isn't anyone here faster, stronger, or deadlier than Bethany Anne. If she believes she needs to be in a fight she will be in it."

Dan spoke up. "Captain Kael-ven T'chmon and myself will fight as called upon, but our role is to get down there and run the operation so you and your warriors will be most effective. What Peter alluded to is that if we don't get our fight in first, we might be the mop-up crew."

Kiel thought for a moment. "Going into battle with Bethany Anne is a race?"

"Uhhh," Dan thought about it for a second, "not so much a race as an opportunity to be a part of one of the deadliest tactical teams in existence."

"But isn't that a bit premature?" Kiel asked. "Don't get me wrong, but you have fought only humans."

"And the ass-kickings your people take when you fight us?" Peter asked.

"We are not in our mech suits during those fights," Kiel argued.

Lance snorted. "Neither is Bethany Anne."

ArchAngel, Queen's Bitches Armory

Jean Dukes and John Grimes each held one side of the black footlocker. It was thirty inches front to back, four feet side to side, and three feet deep.

It weighed close to four hundred pounds.

Jean had worked for the last year with her team on the Queen's latest suit. It was, in Jean's humble opinion, the best one yet. Almost sixty percent more durable and fifteen percent lighter, and still the beautiful deep red.

The color of blood. The color of life.

Together they carried the footlocker into the Bitches' ready room, and with a loud *bang* they dropped it on the floor.

"Fucking shit!" Scott yelled and turned around, his hand on his heart. "Why the fuck did you two have to go and do that?" He looked down at the footlocker, up to them, and down again.

"That," John pointed out to him, "shows you have poor situational awareness."

Scott flipped him off.

"No," Scott retorted, "it shows I place my trust in my teammates not to play asinine pranks that could cause me to go into shock!" He nodded at the box. "This the new set?"

"Yeah," Jean replied as she placed her hand on the lock. The system lights around the rectangle accepted her handprint for verification, blinked twice red, then twice blue, and made a solid *chunk* sound. Jean grabbed the handle and lifted.

Inside were the pieces for Bethany Anne's arms and part of her back. Lower levels in the footlocker held the rest of her equipment.

Scott walked over and looked into the open footlocker. "Sweet." Jean picked up one of the lower arm pieces and handed it to him. "*Damn*, this is light," he murmured as he looked at the armor. He paid attention to the little automated mini-connections that would pull each piece together into a seamless suit. After admiring the work, he looked at Jean. "How much stronger?"

"Sixty percent," she replied.

"That's sure an improvement over two-dot-oh," he agreed. "Guess Tony Stark doesn't have anything on you, huh, Ms. Dukes?"

"Hell, no. That pansy has nothing on me." She put out a hand and Scott gave her back the arm piece. "Except maybe intellect, money, and a seriously fucked-up medical problem with his heart."

Scott looked at John. "We still rocking version two-point-ohs?"

John shook his head. "No, we also have three-point-ohs. They're stronger than our last set, and this time they have three levels of ablative armor."

"Fuck yeah!" Scott grinned and high-fived John. "We are

going to *rock* that joint!" Scott did a little pop dance and spun around to end up back at John and Jean.

John looked back. "You have no idea what I'm talking about, do you?"

Scott laughed, then shrugged. "John, I can't even *spell* 'ablative,' much less confirm what I think it is."

Jean sighed. "Scott, why don't you give me your best shot at what it means?"

Scott folded his arms across his chest, then reached up to scratch his neck. "I'm assuming it is some kind of hardened plastic material that you've spray painted or used other application methodology to protect us against lasers and shit by using vaporization, erosion, and maybe chipping at a controlled rate." He finally stopped scratching his neck to look down at Jean.

Jean's mouth opened and stayed open.

Scott winked at John. "Don't mess with the NYPD SWAT. We just might know what the hell you're talking about."

John snickered until Jean slapped him. "This isn't bros before hos, Mr. Grimes!" She eyed him for a second.

"Sweetie, you should have seen your face. Flies could have landed inside your mouth." He didn't bother to hide his grin.

"Whatever, you two masculine mental midgets." She huffed. "Yes, Scott you are correct. The ablative has been added in case we get more lasers like the drones are seeing in the cave systems. We borrowed some of the technology from defense companies and coupled it with Yollin co-polymer—'

"Stop!" Scott put up a hand. "I concede. Please don't start tossing around chemical names or my masculine-mental-midget mind will explode." He spread his hands apart starting at his ears, mimicking an explosion.

"Hmmmph," she responded. "I'll be nice to you this time. Otherwise Cheryl Lynn might come find me when you can't carry on a conversation for more than twenty seconds without needing a reset."

"Now that you mention it—" Scott started.

"Stop!" This time it was Jean. "I've heard enough from Cheryl Lynn to understand I might not want to know anything past 'reset.' I promise to not explain the chemical makeup of ablative technologies if you promise not to mention anything about what reset entails. Deal?"

Scott shrugged. "Deal."

Jean turned around and Scott winked at John.

Outside Chicago, Illinois, USA

Her worried eyes slid in his direction, so he smiled at her and the girls. It wasn't like he was in control at the moment, but if there was anyone who could help his family leave his home while it was under protection, it was TQB.

He had written four different messages, set to be delivered in —he looked at his watch—fifteen minutes. They should give those who knew him his reasons for doing this. Whether they cared to share the information with the world was another matter.

"Dad, where are we going?" He smiled at his oldest daughter.

"Well, where we will end up is a little vague at the moment, but right now we're going on a trip."

She looked at the small suitcases of clothing their mom told them to bring. "Dad, I don't have near enough clothes if we are going to be gone for longer than," she eyed her suitcase again, "eight hours."

Girls. Indecipherable as teenagers and completely opaque as grown women. Maybe that had to do with the simplicity of men's minds compared to most women. Whoever said boys and girls were the same should have had their head examined for an inability to recognize truth when she bitch-slapped them.

The doorbell rang and he stood up, using a hand gesture to tell his wife and daughters to stay put. His steps echoed as he walked down the ceramic-tiled hallway from the back to the front door. He looked through the peephole, then went back and did it again.

There was a man in a monk's outfit on his stoop.

He opened the door partway and stuck his head out. "Yes?"

The man lifted his hood off his head. "I apologize for the outfit. I haven't had to use it in a long time. My name is Barnabas." He turned and looked over his shoulder, waving at one of the Secret Service detail who had nodded his head in their direction. Barnabas turned back to the ex-President. "I have had discussions with the security here and the two unmarked sedans a little way down the street. They understand you and the family are sneaking out for a movie, and they are here to make sure no one figures out you're gone."

Barnabas raised an eyebrow. "So, may I come in?"

The ex-President nodded and opened the door wider, stepping aside to let this TQB holy man inside. He didn't notice Barnabas releasing a small handful of drones.

Mark Medlin knocked on the front door of the ex-President's house, then glanced at his watch and knocked a little louder.

"I told you, sir. He and his family stepped out for a movie," Agent Terrence Burrow repeated from behind Agent Medlin. The agent had arrived two minutes ago, upset that the ex-President wasn't answering calls from Washington.

And neither was his security team.

Mark turned around. "The ex-President of the United States doesn't just go out and enjoy a movie with his family, not without permission." He knocked louder, but still didn't get a response. "Terrence, open this damned door!" Mark stepped to the side to allow Terrence access.

Terrence shrugged and stepped up. He pulled out his keys

and flipped through them until he had the one for the front door, then reached forward, unlocked the door, and stepped back.

Mark watched him and pressed his lips together. He turned the knob, opened the door and stuck his head inside. "Hello? Anyone home?" He didn't hear any noise from inside.

This couldn't be good.

Terrence waited outside, refusing Mark's request to join him. "It is," Terrence told Mark, "a free country still, right?"

Two minutes later, Mark came out of the house, slamming the front door behind him and talking on the phone, "I don't know where the hell they went! Yes, I got the message they went to the movies, but with whom? They didn't walk. How do I know? Because, dipshit..." Mark kicked a small rock in anger, and it skipped down the driveway, "there are no cars missing!"

ArchAngel, **Operations**

Lance called, "Peter, Todd... A moment, please." The two Queen's Guardians waited while most of those who had been in the meeting filed past them.

Dan was there with the General.

"Sir?" Peter asked, and Todd nodded.

"You need to make sure your guys know to stay behind those who are armored, Peter." Lance told him. "Dan can tell you more, but this is likely going to be a tough operation. Your people are a little too happy to run ahead of the game. Hold them tight this time, got it?"

Peter and Todd nodded, and both answered, "Yes, sir!"

Dulce Lake, New Mexico, USA

Patrick Brown stepped out of the unassuming building and looked around. The main entrance to the facilities below was located in an old-looking rundown metal shed with rust painting the sides off an old highway in some trees.

He had argued for closing it, but Ztopik had effectively over-ruled him. They were to emplace a massive amount of explosives, and when they saw the first few invaders they would let them get into the building and fight their way to the large elevator.

Then the death and mayhem would occur.

Patrick waved to the three guys still installing the explosives and turned around to go inside and back down.

With his recent luck, he would be stuck out here when TQB came calling.

ArchAngel, Medical

Dr. April Keelson walked over to the bed where Anna Elizabeth rested. She had healed, but it was best to monitor the energy usage of the nanocytes for at least twenty-four to forty-eight hours after an event if it was possible. Plus, she was concerned that Anna would have issues after being shot.

The internal trauma to other organs had been bad. While Bethany Anne's nanocytes were certainly some of the best, Anna Elizabeth had still been in terrible shape when she arrived.

"How am I today, Doc?" Anna asked with a bored expression on her face.

"Still want to get out of here?" April asked, and checked the readings.

"Of course! I feel fine." Anna replied. "All I have to do is sit here and read. I'm rather caught up on my reading at the moment, and—"

"And," Bethany Anne cut in and startled both ladies, "you are just as bad at staying still as I am when you believe you're fine. The problem," she told Anna, "is that you have new medical nanites in you. These nanites are using the pathways in your blood to draw energy from the Etheric. These pathways fail eventually, and then they take energy from your blood before they quit working. That draws your energy for personal use down and could, potentially, do more harm than good. You're out of the worst danger, but if you need energy are you ready to drink a cup of blood?"

Bethany Anne's blunt question caught Anna by surprise.

"Did you say, 'Drink a cup of blood?'" she asked, looking at the doctor to see if she would confirm what Bethany Anne had just asked.

Unfortunately, she did.

"Yes," Dr. Keelson agreed. "You will notice the IV. While the hydration and the nutrients are important, it's there to deliver blood if you need it."

"Uh…" Anna looked from the doctor's face to Bethany Anne's and back again. "Well, can I get something to do at least?"

April decided that she would use this explanation the next time someone wanted to leave medical earlier than she thought prudent.

"Sure!" Bethany Anne exclaimed. "As one of my new assistants, you have a lot to catch up on. We'll talk later."

Bethany Anne started walking away, then just disappeared.

Anna, mouth open and eyes shocked, turned to Dr. Keelson. "Did she just say 'assistant?'"

"As a matter of fact she did," April confirmed. She reached into her lab coat and pulled out a slip of paper to hand to Anna. "She told me to give you this if you woke up and she had already left the ship."

Anna unfolded the paper and on it, written in blue ink, was a short message signed by Bethany Anne.

I told you some years ago, you work for me now.

-Bethany Anne

CHAPTER TWENTY-ONE

ArchAngel, **Bethany Anne's Suite**

Bethany Anne pursed her lips and considered what her people were about to do. It would, without a doubt, put them at odds with the United States if the government found out.

Was it worth it?

As far as ADAM and Frank could figure out, this UFO-advanced technology organization was not known to the government at any level. Frank had heard rumors back during the Truman administration in 1947, but he hadn't followed the information too closely. His own work with the UnknownWorld was real, but the idea of aliens was laughable.

Well, who was having the last laugh now?

Certainly not Bethany Anne.

If they encountered technology superior to TQB's, too many of her people would be killed tonight in this raid, but without knowing the challenges they couldn't decide to engage in bombardment on US soil in good conscience. Plus, given the sheer size of the underground cavern system, there was no way for them to know—yet—where they were.

They had found the outside protective details over the last

couple of days, and their drones could not go any further. Team BMW decided that an organic drone might be advisable, but it was impossible to create anything quick enough to support them in this operation.

The choice was now to go in on foot or leave the whole thing for another generation to figure out.

Bethany Anne snorted.

That sounded like the political hacks of just about every country down there. Vote for more taxes and refuse to tackle the hard problems that might get them voted out of office.

"Fucking posers. I won't shirk the hard decisions," she muttered as she walked into her closet. "ArchAngel?"

"Yes?"

"Tell the Bitches to suit up. Tell my father to drop the ships, and remind those on the *G'laxix Sphaea* that they need to drop off the cache of gear in Europe once they're done with Yuko and Akio."

Bethany Anne stripped and grabbed her skinsuit. Her armor had almost everything she needed on the outside of the suit, even special swords and protective scabbards.

Cancer doesn't leave the system peacefully. When you find it, you fight it tooth and nail. The US had a cancer, and it was up to her people to fight it.

She put on the skin booties, then took a step and disappeared.

Bethany Anne stepped out of her receiving chamber, rooms now known as TCs or teleportation chambers, into the armory. She didn't teleport, but it became shorthand for what she did and she had learned to just go with it. The truth was too annoying to beat into everyone's head.

"Hey, look what the cat dragged in!" Darryl called out as he allowed Eric to snap his chest protection into place.

"I'll find a cat to pee in your suit and shut the last lock if you keep that up," she retorted.

"Ooohhh, *gross!*" Darryl's face showed just how distasteful that thought was to him. "Have you *smelled* cat piss?" Bethany Anne tapped the side of her nose. "Yeah, then you know," he told her as he shook his head to try to get rid of the thought.

She nodded and walked over to her footlocker, looking down at it. "So, this is it, huh?"

"Yes," came Jean's muffled voice from behind John. Bethany Anne leaned over to see Jean on the floor with a few tools messing with something on John's left knee.

"Problems?" Bethany Anne asked.

"Fucking second shift failed to reset a catch on the last test and we didn't have any code to catch that failure. I've got to reset fifteen of these cherry-assed twat-muffins before I can reset...the —" There was a loud SNAP and then Bethany Anne saw pins around his knee connection all disconnect, then reconnect and lock in place. "There! That will teach you to fuck with me, you metal mutant," Jean muttered, then she started grabbing her tools and stood up.

Jean smiled like she was about to fire one of the big guns her team had dreamed up. "All right, my Queen, let's get you suited up."

Bethany Anne snickered. You had to love a person who enjoyed their job and was made for it. Bethany Anne was pretty sure Jean Dukes' name was going to be admired on a lot of worlds.

If they weren't too busy cussing her out.

NORAD, US

The North American Aerospace Defense Command (NORAD) is a United States and Canada bi-national organization charged with the missions of aerospace warning and aerospace control for North America. They had been having fits trying to track TQB ships for the past four years.

Now they had incredibly sensitive tools that someone quipped could find a pimple on a bird's ass.

As always, they were on alert to see who might spot a TQB incursion. Since no TQB-requested flights were on tonight's report, it would be a feather in anyone's cap to be the first to find and confirm an unapproved approach.

Days later, NORAD's best would be going through the recordings from this evening to figure out how they had missed all the activity, because apparently TQB hadn't been trying to stay off the radar before and NORAD had no idea just how good TQB's new anti-radar truly was.

NORAD might be able to spot a pimple on a bird's ass, but apparently they couldn't spot over twenty massive shipping container-sized ships dropping from space toward New Mexico.

At least not when TQB didn't want them to.

ArchAngel, Three Hundred Miles above New Mexico

General Lance Reynolds watched the incoming data from the drones and the ships that had landed. There were three landing zones that split up those heading into the cave system. They had figured out the likely main entrance to the base, but Lance told everyone not to focus on that location. The main entrance would be well defended or well protected somehow.

That didn't mean they would ignore it. On the contrary, once the drone confirmed their suspicions they would have a very small group strike up top.

Carefully.

Twenty minutes later, ArchAngel verified Lance's suspicions. "General, we have confirmation from our drones that there is explosive residue outside the main entrance."

"How far outside the front door?" Lance asked as he nodded

to a support person to bring up the three dimensional view of the building.

"Up to thirty-three meters, sir," ArchAngel replied. An orange line started drawing itself around the hologram as the drones figured out where new dirt had been unearthed. Twice the drones had sniffed unknown chemicals. The mix was something ArchAngel didn't have the characteristics for in her database.

"ADAM?" Lance called.

"Yes, sir?" he replied.

"Do you have anything on those two unknown chemicals?" he asked, highlighting the two rows of data.

"One moment, General."

Almost two minutes later, ADAM came back. "I have spoken with Yollin Scientist Royleen, and he has tentatively identified that chemical makeup as an explosive used for mining operations. Depending on the quantity, he says to stay at least a hundred meters away from it."

"A hundred fucking meters?" Lance was shocked. "Shit." He saw ADAM draw a circle a hundred meters around both targets directly on opposing sides of the building. "That would kill everything inside the building and outside as well," he commented.

Lance looked again and pointed out two areas in the hologram. "I bet you the drones have missed two more locations equidistant from these two locations. Basically the four poles in a circle." Lance muttered it to himself, but ArchAngel took it as a command.

"Checking, General," she replied. Less than a minute later the EI confirmed the two additional locations.

Lance wanted to spit, but there was nowhere to do so in his operations room. "Dammit, if we go knocking on this front door it's going to be blown away." He grabbed a cigar and unwrapped it, then stuck it in his mouth unlit to chew on.

"ArchAngel, patch me in to Dan."

Immediately he had Dan on the comm. "This is Dan."

Lance got right to the point. "Dan, ArchAngel is downloading data about new chemical traces we found up near the main entrance. Make sure the drones and other chemical sniffers know it and mark it. Royleen says to stay a hundred meters away from this shit."

"Wow, that bad?" Dan asked.

"Yes, and more so for you guys underground. He says it looks like mining explosives," Lance explained.

"Well, fuck." Dan replied. "Understood, and thanks."

Lance changed channels. "Bethany Anne?"

"Here," she replied.

"ETA?" he asked. He had barely finished his request when a holographic digital timer, counting down, appeared in his operations tank.

Two minutes till midnight.

Captain Kael-ven T'chmon, First of the Yollin Mercenary Group "DeathBringers," turned when he saw Kiel look up.

He smiled. Bethany Anne's new dropship design for his people was very nice. It took into account both those in mech suits and those without, such as himself. They were locked into the Etheric Empire's communication comm suite and if he were honest with himself...

It was frightening.

These humans knew war, and they knew it like a species designed by the gods for it. If these humans had been—or could be—roped into fighting for one of the seven Kurtherian Clans? Well, perhaps he and his people needed to support Bethany Anne.

Because with Kurtherian technology he wasn't sure he knew of a species that could best them even if their whole world was involved.

It was a problem now. For his species to survive, did he need to make sure this woman would be able to defeat his own people?

Kael-ven pushed the concern aside and focused as the dark-crimson-painted dropship slowed to a stop. The ship had her vampire-skull design painted on the side and a zero one beside it.

The door opened, and Kiel mumbled a particularly impressive set of Yollin expletives. Bethany Anne jumped off the dropship and her men followed her, all of them in their mech suits. The suits didn't rely on massive motors for speed and power like theirs, but instead used Kurtherian Etheric-driven motors that were much smaller, allowing for more refined suits.

Kiel turned to his captain. "I will give up my whole pay for this operation if they will build me a set."

Captain Kael-ven turned to his military leader. "Are you speaking ahead of yourself?"

Kiel shook his head. "Captain," he nodded toward the humans "I'm military through and through, and I *need* one of those suits." Agreements were muttered behind Kiel as his people, in their own suits, grumbled. They went from being the Mighty Yollin Mechanized Unit with advanced suits and abilities to feeling like they received their mech-suits from the used spaceship yard on the third moon of Asht'rix.

And everyone knew you didn't trust anything that came from Asht'rix without checking it out.

Twice.

"Told you," came a male human voice from behind them.

Captain Kael-ven and his people turned to see Peter and two of his men behind them. "Tonight, you guys," Peter nodded to the few females in the group, "and ladies, are going to find out what it is like to fight behind the most fucking badass leader in the galaxy."

"Aren't you getting in a suit, Guardian Peter?" Kiel asked.

"Oh, I am," Peter told him, "but it isn't good for me to hold my form just sitting around doing nothing."

"You are going to *change* and then get into a mechanized suit?" Kiel asked, shock plainly evident as his mandibles hung open.

"Kiel," Peter shook his head, "how the hell do you think I plan on keeping up with my Queen?" He laughed. "Dude, you are about to go on the operation of your life. Trust me."

Peter started undressing and the two guys next to him opened the cases they had brought. "She's here, so I won't try to go off the reservation now." He twisted his neck left and something popped. He did the same thing to the right. Then his voice went deeper. "It's time to take the fight to the enemies of my *Queen!*"

Kiel wanted to take a step back as the huge Pricolici suddenly stood in front of him, his piercing eyes yellow in the dim light, watching him like prey.

The two men next to Peter quickly started yanking components and fitting the Pricolici, who was impatiently waiting for them to get the suit on him.

Kiel watched as Peter's men put on the armor, then turned to his captain as if to say, "Even *he* gets the special armor!"

Peter had started growling when another, deeper growl emanated from behind him. "Peterrr!" Nathan's voice was deep and malevolent. Already in his form, he walked into the circle. In his jet-black mech suit with a paw print on his left breastplate he finished his threat, "Sttannnd orrr Iii willl mmake yooouuu stanndd."

Peter stopped growling as the last three pieces of armor were locked in place, and bent down for them to lock on his helmet.

Bethany Anne, helmet off, walked over with her team and Dan following behind. "Are my Yollin mercenaries ready?" There was a sparkle of amusement in her eyes.

"No," Captain Kael-ven replied. "It seems we are having mech-suit envy, and their minds are not on the operation."

Bethany Anne pursed her lips. "We finish this operation, and depending on how you perform we will talk, Captain Kael-ven. Amaze me and we will upgrade your suits." She nodded to him and his people, then she and her team continued walking toward the large cave entrance.

Dan stopped next to Captain Kael-ven as the Yollins followed Bethany Anne and the two Pricolici into the darkness.

Kael-ven looked down at Dan. "Did she just take my people's heart?" he asked as he noticed his team standing a little straighter and listening perhaps a little more closely.

"Yup," Dan answered. "Welcome to my world, Kael-ven."

Ztopik had never adjusted to the wake-and-sleep cycle of these humans. He might spend days awake on his research, only to go to sleep for the same amount of time when done.

His body required approximately a one-in-five ratio of sleep-to-wake time. For him, it wasn't sleep so much as reducing his mental processes enough to allow his mind the rest it needed. He would dim the lights and choose a simple problem to consider as he spent the time restoring the energy necessary for his brain to operate efficiently.

Helping the humans with the trap above had been a little challenging, since he hadn't worked with that type of science in a very long time. Unfortunately, he'd had to mix the chemicals. If he had tried to use the slaves to accomplish this, there was a good chance it would have destroyed a perfectly useable room within his level inside the base.

Then, he would have had to suffer additional humans in his domain and that would be...distasteful.

They always created trouble, and the last time some of them had worked in level six it had required an extermination event for both a quarter of his slaves and another sixty humans.

A waste of good slaves, not to happen again if he could help it.

Once this problem with the potential threat was overcome, he should consider replacing Patrick Brown and Eva Hocks.

Their effectiveness over the last few years had dropped, this present situation with TQB being a prime example. Patrick hiding information that Ztopik needed to continue with his plans could not be allowed to continue.

Ztopik flipped the page over and finished writing his thoughts. A few moments later, he stopped writing and watched as the ink faded. The information was now stored in the secondary crystal and could be reviewed at any time.

He set down the writing instrument and started walking toward the exit. A few steps from the door, he heard a beep.

Ztopik turned slowly and his lips drew together.

There were alarms going off for the lower, not upper, levels.

CHAPTER TWENTY-TWO

Half a Mile inside Entrance Three, Dulce Lake, New Mexico, USA

"I'm telling you I smell something." Sadhi told Ken as the two of them worked their way left around a large outcropping with the rest of the team behind them. The minimal light their helmets projected was all that was needed to help the two Wechselbalg see well in the dark.

Ken put up a hand and his group of six stopped. He breathed deeply a couple of times. He didn't want to stop right now. After the ass-chewing he and Sadhi received from Peter for their failure to recognize the Queen, he was really hoping to make a good impression on this operation.

Being cowards and jumping at every little sound or bad feeling wasn't going to get them to the base.

He pulled up his tablet and tapped the command to have a drone come to their area and confirm the next hundred yards.

Being dead wasn't going to get them to the base. He gave them a hand signal, and they took up positions looking out. Moments later, three of the group turned their heads when a tiny insect went through them to check their path.

The seconds seemed to crawl by for Ken, who was belittling his own decision when his tablet vibrated. The map showing his path had been updated. He and his team had been re-routed around their original path, and the area ahead of them had been marked off with a skull-and-crossbones symbol.

He slid the tablet back into this pocket. "Sadhi!"

"Sir?" came the response.

"You and your golden fucking nose get up front. You just saved all our damned lives." Ken told the rest of the group, "Let's keep going, but Sadhi is now smelling ahead of us. There are explosives in front of us, people."

Bethany Anne and her team jumped from location to location down their entrance. She had decided, over the objections of just about everyone, that she and the Bitches were going first. Dan sent multiple drones ahead of her team and additional drones stayed with them.

There was no way base personnel would be able to miss her arrival, and that was her plan. If they had military resources, the people in the mech-suits had the best chance to live through it.

"Kiel!" hissed Bo'cha'tien over their personal suit comm. "This woman is crazy!" She laughed as they jumped over a large pit. Their suit lights allowed them to see in the utterly dark cave as if it were twilight.

The two Yollins were the closest to the five humans in front of them. The team was rushing through the cave system like Kolleens on Th'Reek crystals. The two Pricolicis were just ahead and to the side of them. They were apparently wave number two.

"Yes!" Kiel replied, exultation in his voice. "Peter said we would need to keep up, and I thought him to be telling a small untruth!" Kiel looked at the path ahead. The cave opened wider, and had a much higher roof. He jacked up the power and boosted, easily clearing a seventy-foot section of the path and leapfrogging the two Pricolici, who growled their annoyance at his sudden advance.

Bo'cha'tien laughed. "That is cheating!"

Kiel didn't answer, just focused on keeping his speed up as they dashed around a corner. He trusted those in front of him to warn him about problems ahead.

Now was time to race!

"Prepare for war, Bo'cha'tien, for we rush to seize it in our crushing grip and strangle those who will not yield to us!" Kiel slipped on a rock and his suit bounced hard off the wall. He straight-armed a pillar of rock on his left to get back on track, but Peter had caught up.

"Iii tollldd youu, Kieellll!" The sinewy monster next to him laughed. "It is for us to be warriors and race to that which we were *born to do!*"

Every being in their mechanical suits heard Bethany Anne's shout of joy as they rushed through the caves, "Catch up to me, my people, for today we *WILL KICK EVERY ASS WE SEE!*"

"*WHAT THE HELL IS COMING AT US?*" Patrick yelled over the video connection in his operations room to Ztopik, who had never left his own.

"Your yelling, Lead Operations Patrick, is not conducive to effective leadership," Ztopik replied tersely. He was watching Bethany Anne's team get closer, the system registering their approximate position from seismic calculations and occasional snippets of video.

The lasers in the system were useless. They barely had time to fire one, maybe two shots before something took them out.

"Get your people to the bottom level, Lead Operations

Patrick, or we will have no one protecting us from below," Ztopik commanded.

"How the hell do they know the caves?" Patrick bitched, keeping himself from yelling in his frustration. "We would have seen any humans or…"

Patrick's voice dropped off. Ztopik presumed Patrick had figured out a possibility. For Ztopik, the "how" didn't matter at this point.

It just *was*.

One didn't argue with reality, not when the proof was coming straight toward them.

"Should we bring back XJ-02?" Patrick asked.

"No," Ztopik responded. "If we need support above, they will be there for you. I doubt this group hasn't planned for fighting the ships inside the caverns."

Patrick hated asking Ztopik for help, but he had to admit he had been waging a silent fight with TQB for the past few years.

And his failure was staring him in his face as TQB raced through the cave system straight at him.

Ztopik sent out a mental command, then, "I will provide support. Tell your people to not interfere with my Grays."

Patrick nodded and Ztopik cut the connection.

"We have light ahead," Bethany Anne reported. "It's time to fly, folks."

Having made their best effort to spring any traps in their path, Bethany Anne and her team slowed to a stop to wait for the Pricolici and the Yollins to catch up. When they arrived Bethany Anne asked Kiel, "Do you use this same tactic?"

"This leapfrogging?" Kiel asked. "No. Our suits are usually more advanced than those of the enemy we fight, so we haven't had to do this."

"Well, we have an enemy of unknown ability and another alien somewhere in there," Bethany Anne told everyone. "I want it thinking."

Bo'cha'tien smiled. "You want it thinking Yollins are attacking?" The Yollin female's eyes narrowed. She liked that they would be the first into view.

"Hell, yes, so you'll be dropping in first. Start making a mess to get their attention. When we get enough of their defense to show up, we'll leapfrog you and drop in."

"What do we do at that point?" Kiel asked.

"Whatttt weeee plannn tooo dooo allll nnnightttt," Peter answered. "Ccatch uup."

Round disks arrived above all of those in suits, each with two bars on the bottom. As the disks positioned themselves above those standing, they would reach up and grab the bars. The controls were simple.

Bethany Anne looked around. "Time to earn your money, DeathBringers!"

With a bone-vibrating chittering, the six Yollins rose into the air and headed toward the large flat area ahead of them.

"Ready, Bitches?" Bethany Anne asked, looking around. She added, "And Nathan."

His guttural laughter reverberated off the rock walls as another seven armor-encased bodies lifted into the cavern's darkness.

Patrick's face popped back up on Ztopik's screen. "What are *those*, Ztopik?" His voice was half-angry, half-frustrated because the enemy was now in view of their high-powered video cameras.

And Patrick had no idea what was in the large and obviously non-human mechanized suits as they dropped down right outside the landing field.

There was no mistaking the opening conversation with the aliens. They unlimbered guns and started shooting anything that looked like it was valuable.

They weren't here to play nice.

"Those," Ztopik answered, anger flooding his carefully-cultured voice, "are Yollins!"

His mind raced. Ztopik could not figure out how Yollins could be, or even why they would be, attacking them. They should have fifty ships in orbit and simply deliver an ultimatum.

Patrick spoke commands to another screen, and Ztopik could now hear the crack of normal weapons fire from the men Patrick had hastily moved to the lower levels.

"Those guns are not going to accomplish anything against the Yollins." Ztopik paused, sending mental commands to his slaves. "My Grays are arriving now. They will even up the fight."

The constant pinging of projectile weapons hitting Kiel's suit was annoying as hell, but the bullets didn't present a danger to him or his people. Each time a face, leg, or arm showed itself, half a dozen bolts either blew it apart or damaged the area it had just been in.

Bo'cha'tien spoke privately, "Why are we hiding?"

"Because our employer told us to, Bo'cha'tien," he replied.

"Well, I think this is stupid," she told him. "It is obvious that these humans have nothing that can hurt us. Watch!"

Kiel turned in time to see Bo'cha'tien jump out from behind her protection and start shooting randomly. She drew attention from Kiel, and the heavy patter of bullets on his armor lessened. His order for her to return to her protection was lost as she yelled over her loudspeaker.

"Eat Yollin plasma and die, *MOTHERFUCKERS!*"

Sam Bollard was pissed. Despite its heavier bullet, his M14 wasn't doing shit to these aliens, but, at the moment it was what he had. The alien bastards stayed behind the outcroppings just outside the flattened landing area and their return fire had already killed three of his people.

Then, one of the aliens jumped out and started blasting heavy bolts of hot shit everywhere. It started chittering over a loud-speaker on its suit. No one could understand anything but the two words at the end.

Greg yelled over to him, "Did that alien just say 'die mother-fuckers?'"

"Yeah!" Sam confirmed. "Who the fuck is teaching them English?"

Goowek sent out the command, "Place all debilitation devices on max power. We are not acquiring specimens. We are commanded to kill these Yollins."

The five Grays with him checked their weapons and dialed each of the three settings to max. While they had fewer shots...

Each would be powerful.

When the elevator opened, Goowek and his team stepped out. They emptied into a short hallway that led to the landing cave, where two men were using their weapons from the exit. He and his people were not fast, but what they lacked in speed...

They made up in firepower.

He walked calmly toward the opening.

"HAHAHAHAHA... Kiss my Yollin ass, you pink hairless bunnies!" Bo'cha'tien yelled, slamming two more shots toward the large rock two of the men were hiding behind.

Bethany Anne's voice came over the system, "We have aliens, we have *aliens!*"

Kiel twisted to look and saw a short Zeta Reticulan step into view just inside one of the entrances. He lifted his hand and aimed, then...

"Bo'cha'tien, look out!" Kiel shouted. He jacked up his power and shoved off the ground. Time seemed to stop as he jumped at Bo'cha'tien's legs. He could see brightness to his left before his visor darkened.

Ztopik watched the screen to monitor what was going on. A Yollin just stood there accepting the human weapons fire and playing with the humans, then another jumped toward the one in the open.

Ztopik calculated the timing and wondered at the outcome.

"We have aliens, we have *aliens!*" came over Bo'cha'tien's communicator. She looked around, surprised to hear Bethany Anne's voice, and then saw the Zeta Reticulan. It was a short Gray, its unblinking eye aiming a...

"Oh, shit!"

Sometimes humans had the best words for a situation. She had already used "motherfucker" and now she had to cross off "shit," too.

Her desire to get out and prove herself had finally gotten her killed.

Fuck my life.

She started turning her gun, because who knew? Maybe they would miss. Maybe they…

SLAM!

Her body violently rocketed to the side, having been smashed into by something from her left. That was when her suit's alarms all went to yellows and reds.

Before she blacked out, she noted that her left arm was listed as red with a mark through it.

The drugs hit her system and kept her body from going into shock, and she had a passing thought as her thoughts dimmed.

"I've lost my arm."

"Move, Bitches." The command came from Bethany Anne, and she and her team, who had been holding steady at the top of the cave out of sight, dropped down quickly via the grav carriers. Twenty feet from the floor they let go.

Seven bodies encased in the world's most advanced mechanized armor dropped into the midst of the defenders, with Bethany Anne landing just to the side of the hallway opening.

Goowek had been watching to see if he could get another shot at the two Yollins who had disappeared behind the rock on his left, since he didn't have enough power to shoot indiscriminately.

He barely had time to register the deep-red-armored person before his head exploded.

Fractions of a second later his five team members had also been targeted and killed.

"Kiel!" Bethany Anne called.

"Here," his voice replied over the comm.

"How is Bo'cha'tien?" she asked. She looked to her left, where a man was pulling up a pistol to shoot her, so she grabbed it out of his hand. Crumpling it up, she tossed it away. He reached back for the rifle he had been using a moment before, and she reached down to her leg. She issued a command and one piece separated. She used the armor-sized wakizashi to cut the man's head off before she reattached the sword. "Stupid ass," she muttered as she walked toward the elevator.

Kiel came back, "She will live, but the weapon disintegrated her whole arm."

"No shit?" Bethany Anne walked back to the first alien, then picked up the weapon it had used and pushed it into the Etheric.

As she strode past the five other bodies, she picked up every one of their weapons and pushed them into the Etheric as well. Better to not leave this technology hanging around.

"Folks," she put out over the radio, "the little gray guys have something that will disintegrate you, so if you see one of those put it down fast. Grab the weapon, though. I want them for R&D." She switched to the command channel. "You got that, Dan?"

Dan's voice came back, "Watch out for the little gray guys, their weapons will atomize you."

"That's right. And we have a Yollin down. She's missing her arm," Bethany Anne stated. "So let's get this going, but make sure everyone is super-careful."

"John's going to be particularly happy about this," Dan quipped.

Bethany Anne thought about it. "You know, that's not a bad suggestion."

He agreed, "I know. It's why you pay me the big bucks, Bethany Anne."

She watched as her guys took a few moments to check everything out and get their stuff back together. "Okay, bring up the teams, Dan."

"We have a problem with Entrance Three," he reported.

"What problem?"

"Their paths are totally blocked by explosives. We're pulling them out, putting up a puck curtain, and moving them to entrance two at this time, but they'll be a couple minutes behind."

"Any change on the Pods flying in here for cover?"

"Nope, we still have something messing up the computers on the Pods. Until that stops, we are stuck."

Bethany Anne looked at the elevator. "It's like the damned scene in Star Wars where we have to turn off the tractor beam," she huffed. "Okay, keep them coming. We have to deal with this elevator."

"Good luck." Dan closed the connection.

Bethany Anne looked at her guys. "Who's feeling lucky?"

All of the guys glanced at each other as Kiel walked up. Great. Now she had seven males of two species looking at her.

"Okay, anyone who wants to volunteer, take a step forward."

Six sets of feet shuffled one step backward.

Kiel turned and looked behind him. The guys were all smiling, and he turned back around to see Bethany Anne smiling at him as well.

Except...her smile seemed just a touch malicious.

Kiel looked down at his feet and then everyone else's feet and realized he was now in front of everyone else. He turned back to Bethany Anne. "I want it on the record that I have been screwed."

Bethany Anne reached out to him. "Sorry. I can only take one with me, and you just volunteered."

"Take me whe..." the Yollin got out before they both disappeared.

The humans laughed softly in the sudden silence before they spread out to make sure no one took them by surprise.

CHAPTER TWENTY-THREE

The MJ-12 operations room was full of people. Patrick had a team watching all video cameras, but really focusing on the ones that showed the elevator and elevator shaft. More of his people were busy setting up explosives they could drop down the shaft.

The final descent to the bottom landing field was through a hundred and twenty feet of damn near impregnable rock.

Patrick's eyes narrowed and he hit the buttons to switch through the video streams from outside. So far TQB had destroyed twelve of their cameras, but they still had four in operation.

TQB had not brought any devices that could dig through rock as far as he could determine. He jerked a little when the video stream that he was watching suddenly went to static.

Make that three video cameras still in operation.

He gritted his teeth. They had made defensive preparations up top, but not nearly enough down at the bottom. They were between a rock and a hard place, and the final choice he had was to call in the US military.

But if he did that, they would be screwed a second time. A few or even most of his people might get away, but there was no way the experiments in Section Two could be allowed to leave.

Or even be found.

Patrick was watching the video stream of the team working to booby-trap the elevator shaft when his brain could not...no, *dared* not believe what his eyes were telling him.

Etheric

"What...is this place?" Kiel asked, taking in the amorphous gray landscape. The light was bright enough, but because of thick fog he couldn't see. The sensors of his mech suit were not helping either.

Bethany Anne chuckled. "Follow me. This is the Etheric dimension. We can't travel too far, because between the two of us, the energy to transfer this much metal drains me every damned step we take." Even now he could start to hear her breathing harder.

"Where are we going, and how far is it?" Kiel asked as he looked around, trying to get a sense of where he was.

"Fuck if I know, but it had better not be too far." She stopped and leaned forward just a bit, and then they continued another five paces before she stopped and leaned forward again.

"What are you doing?" Kiel finally asked.

"Looking out from inside the elevator shaft to figure out if we're at a floor yet," she answered and then resumed walking. She did this three more times before pausing longer. "Oh... Well, that's just fucking rude."

"What?" Kiel asked.

Bethany Anne looked up and around wherever she was looking before she reached back to him. "Hold my hand and walk three steps with me."

Kiel gently grasped her mech suit's hand and paced himself with her shorter strides. She continued holding his hand and leaned forward again. "Oh, this is going to be delicious," she murmured.

"Are you planning on eating something?" Kiel asked.

"What?" She straightened. "No. At least, I hope not. I need you to go take care of some humans in the real world." She looked around. "I've got to rest for a few minutes and pull in energy. I'm sorry to tell you this, but you are a real fuck-ton of energy-sucking alien to be yanking through the Etheric." She turned to him. "Ready to be a scary alien mercenary and kill some people?"

Eric and Darryl were standing near the elevator when both turned toward it in unison.

"You heard that?" Eric asked and Darryl agreed.

"Screaming, yelling, and a few..." Darryl stopped speaking. A shriek of terror seemed to be approaching fast.

The sudden *thump/splat* was loud and clear to the both of them. Darryl looked uneasy.

Someone had just decided to fall down the elevator shaft.

Darryl called over the comm, "Hey, folks, I think Team Bethany Anne just let us know they're clearing out the path up above us."

Peter came up to them and sniffed the air. "Fresh dead. She isn't leaving anyone for us." He heaved a huge sigh of frustration. "Why didn't I step forward?"

Kiel was trying to take these new experiences in stride, including when she told him to take a step forward and he went from being in the Etheric fog to inside a base in a hallway hewn out of rock.

With seven humans in front of him arrayed around an open elevator door. He could see the empty shaft beyond. He took a step and grabbed the right arm of a man with a rifle. When he tossed him forward, the flying body knocked one guy near the elevator entrance out of the way. The body continued through the opening and slammed into the far wall of the elevator shaft. Kiel could hear him screaming as he descended, until his sudden stop ended any of his worries.

Forever.

Kiel cranked his suit's power up and within seven-point-two human seconds he had been shot with forty-two rounds, three of which ricocheted and hit other humans. For him it wasn't a problem. Three humans died of crushed skulls, two of crushed chests, and one arm had come off when he forgot to adjust his suit's power back down before he threw him. He remembered a phrase one of Bethany Anne's people had used, and he murmured it as he tossed the arm away. "Oops, my bad."

That human was screaming as he lay on the floor, so Kiel casually kicked his head to shut him up. Then, inside his helmet, he made a face when he got brains on the end of his mech suit's foot.

"Gahh!" He took a step and felt the organic matter between his boot and the floor for a couple steps before it rubbed off. "I've got to remember that those heads are crunchy on the outside but meaty on the inside."

His eyes opened when an arm appeared from thin air in front of him and pushed him backward.

He landed on his ass in the Etheric fog again.

"Nice job, now come along. I found their operations room." She started walking in a different direction from before. Her steps seemed a little slower.

Kiel got up and walked with her. He got a warning beep that his energy was down fifty percent.

It seemed *her* energy wasn't the only thing the Etheric drained.

Patrick was staring at the video input when the back of a Yollin attacker appeared in the middle of his video feed.

"What the fuck?" He jerked back when he saw the Yollin fighter grab Greg Humble and throw him into the elevator shaft. Greg disappeared.

The sounds of gunfire came through the speakers as well as screams of the men as they turned to fight the alien who had somehow snuck up behind them.

In seconds it was over. The Yollin kicked Jay Biers in the head and crushed his skull. As it took steps toward the video camera, an arm appeared and the alien fell backward, then disappeared. All Patrick could see now were the dead bodies in the hallway outside the elevator.

"Kenny!" he yelled. Hearing Kenny's 'Sir?' he ordered, "Lock down this room!" He opened the top drawer of his desk and then slammed it shut, opening the second in a rush. He pulled out a silver-gray metal container with a place for his thumb. When he pressed the lock it turned green, and he used both hands to open the box. With the box still in his right hand, he pulled out Ztopik's gift to him.

His own Zeta weapon. He placed the box on the desk and turned toward the door, keeping an eye on the video cameras in case the alien attacked somewhere else.

Bethany Anne was leaning forward. "Yeah, this is the place." She pulled back and sat down before finally lying on the ground. She reached up and unhooked her helmet, taking it off.

Kiel was surprised to see that her face had lost most of its color. Her skin was now almost the color of bones bleached in the sun of many seasons.

"What can I do?" Kiel asked, concerned she was going to die. If she did, how was he going to explain this to the rest of the team?

Hell, how was he going to get out of this dimension? He unlatched his helmet and took it off, sniffing the air.

"Give me a few more seconds. I am barely pulling in energy right now. If you can shut down your systems, do so. I need enough energy to push you through, then you need to stay alive long enough for me to get in and help you."

"Why would I not be alive?" Kiel asked, shutting down unnecessary systems in his suit.

"This is the operations room," she told him. "There are a lot of people in there. Probably not as many rifles, but I'm sure there are lots of pistols and high-ranking staff."

She closed her eyes for a moment, then took a deep breath and then stood up, "If anyone is going to have weapons we don't like, it's going to be them."

Kiel considered his options. "How big is the room?" She told him, and he turned off the ability to jump high and drained the energy back out of those capacitors into his plasma gun. "Do you need any of the machines in there?"

She was silent for a moment. "Yes, probably."

The Yollin's two mandible-looking appendages turned inward at the top, then straightened. He drained the energy from the plasma pistols and looked at his supply of kinetic rounds. "How many people?"

She paused, then leaned forward, then pulled back. "About forty-two."

"I've got seventy kinetics left." He pulled that pistol and exchanged the magazine for a full load.

"Don't waste your shots," she advised.

Fortunately Kiel was able to bite back his response. He wasn't sure what the translation software would have told her, but in his language it was pretty damned disrespectful. He decided to just nod in her general direction instead.

She put her helmet back on and he followed her lead. "Let's do this."

"One second." He turned away from her. "Okay, I take a tiny step and you push, correct?"

"Yes," she agreed. "You're coming out in a corner of the room where there are no people or furniture. I'll look right before I push you. Everyone is going to be in front and to your left, I think."

"You think?" Kiel asked.

She barked, "Step!"

The first person to die in front of Patrick was Michael Shanks. His head shattered, coating those around him in blood and brain matter.

The ones who had been shot but were not dead started screaming as Patrick dropped and scanned the room. An alien in the back-left corner of the room was calmly shooting his people.

Patrick flicked off the safety on his disintegrator and aimed it at the alien, who was turning toward him.

There would be only one chance to get this shot right.

"*FUCK YOUUUU!*" Patrick yelled, but then it was his turn to scream in pain when a sword cut through his arm. The disintegrator beam took a chunk out of the rock ceiling between him and the alien.

Patrick barely had time to recognize that his arm was gone before a metal kinetic round blew through his chest, tossing his now-dead body like a rag doll over the desk behind him.

"This is BA," she commed. "Status?"

"Bored," John answered. "You planning on letting us in there?"

"Damn, you lazy-butt whale-sniffing asshats haven't found another way through tons of rock?" she replied, to the men's amusement.

"No, but we think the elevator shaft might be haunted," Darryl replied. "It's raining dead people."

She laughed. "Kiel didn't send him down dead."

"Well, he *finished* dead," Eric answered.

"We've got video, and the elevator shaft is clear. They were setting up a loud boom for you if you came up the elevator, and as far as I can tell that is the only path up. Take it up one floor, and then you have stairs that access the floor above. Seven floors total. I'm on three."

"Anything else we should know?" John asked as he pointed to himself, Nathan, and Scott for the first elevator test.

"Yeah," she came back, voice calm. "There's another elevator shaft and I don't have any video in that section."

"Understood," John replied and the connection went silent.

Darryl quipped, "That's not, like, *ominous* or anything."

Ztopik watched as the humans died in the operations room, his little mouth pursed. The Yollin was calmly and efficiently shooting them. He would not have to worry about dealing with Patrick before putting a replacement in charge.

"Meehine," he pointed toward the secondary exit, "go to the research lab and prepare to release the fourth wave."

The little gray alien obediently turned and headed toward the research floor.

How did the Yollins get through Patrick's defenses?

John, Nathan, and Scott stepped into the elevator and John pushed the button for level three.

The three men, two in human mech-suits and one in a Pricolici suit, waited for the elevator to rise.

"Sure wish we had some music," Scott grumbled. "Hell, I'd even take Barry Manilow right now." Nathan snickered behind him.

"Not exactly music to take over an alien base by," John commented.

"Well, neither is this dead air," Scott said when the elevator slowed to a stop.

"Wonnndeerrr hhhoowww wee finnddd herrr," Nathan growled.

The doors opened and the men heard gunfire down the hallway. John stabbed the button for the elevator to go back down to the lowest level. "Follow the audio crumbs of destruction and chaos."

The three of them ran down the hallway.

"Bethany Anne, I'm running out of ammunition!" Kiel called.

"Don't worry about it," she replied.

"We don't know if they have more of those weapons!" Kiel retorted. When the ceiling had lost a chunk Kiel realized he had almost become the Yollin Mercenary Company's first death.

"It's not about that," Bethany Anne corrected. "It's about…"

The roar reverberated down the hallway and poured into the room. The gunshots coming into the room had stopped, but gunshots aimed elsewhere continued.

Then there were screams of terror and bodies getting ripped apart or slamming into walls.

Bethany Anne put down her sword. "Okay guys, don't say we didn't save some for you."

"*Fuck!*" Scott called back. "Did you have to get them all worked up?"

"Stttoppp youourrr bitttchhhinggg!" Nathan growled. His laughter sounded pretty damned evil when it accompanied the dismemberment of humans, whose cries were suddenly silenced.

"Fine!" Scott yelled back. "Don't say I wasn't polite."

Kiel walked to the doorway, peeked around and saw the huge Pricolici with a human in his left hand who was trying to beat his arm as he dangled in the air. Nathan squeezed his neck, and a loud *snap* preceded him dropping the dead body. Nathan grabbed the face of another human with his right hand, and that one's scream of pain ended suddenly with the shattering of his skull. "He hee hehhhehe."

Soon there were no more humans opposing them.

Bethany Anne walked into the hallway and spoke to the guys, "Remind me to tell Ashur I'm sorry. I could have used his furry ass on this operation."

"We need to look after the Queen. She is weak," Kiel insisted as he came out of the room.

Bethany Anne turned around. "You just fucking ratted me out!" She bitched at Kiel. "*Gott Verdammt!* The alien mercenaries are stabbing me in the back!"

Ztopik watched the humans and the non-humans kill the Majestic-12 people. He considered options and then his tiny mouth turned up. He pressed three buttons and all the computers in the room shut down.

Turning around, he headed toward his research level.

There was no time like the present, he thought, to determine which of his creations was the deadliest.

It took the teams twenty minutes to run through the rest of the levels. Those humans who gave up were rounded up and taken back to the caves.

If they fought, they were eliminated.

Bethany Anne and her team found the scientists shaking in their offices. Peter brought a female to her. "Thisss isss tttheee heeeaddd doctorrr."

Bethany Anne, her helmet in her hands, turned to look at the woman. She had mascara streaks that tears must have made, but at the moment, she glared at Bethany Anne.

"You bitch!" she hissed, "You have killed my friends here...for what?"

"You tried killing my people first," Bethany Anne retorted.

The scientist spat, "We are trying to make the US the most advanced superpower in the world. What are you doing?"

"Saving the world from aliens, you self-centered, poor excuse for a human being." Bethany Anne replied, then handed Eric her helmet. "I don't have time, and she isn't worth my pity."

"What are you doing?" The scientist started fighting Peter's hold, trying to kick backward. "Stay away from me!" Her foot found his armor and she cried out in pain.

Bethany Anne's eyes turned red. "Hello Dr. Eva Hocks." Her voice dripped disgust. "I was wrong. You aren't a poor excuse for a human being. You aren't a human being."

"What are you doing?" Dr. Hocks looked at each man. "Stop her!"

John spoke up. "BA, you need me to slap her if she speaks?"

"Iiii cannn biiiitte herrrr," Peter offered.

Dr. Hocks was twisting for all she was worth, but it barely budged Peter's arms. Her pleading became crying.

"You seek knowledge above everything." Bethany Anne's head turned to the side. "You have experimented on humans."

Dr. Hocks, tears spilling, noticed that her eyes, which had

previously held no emotions toward her, now looked at her with judgment.

A thought made its way through all the emotion. She wasn't getting out of this alive. She felt something digging through her mind.

"Where are the two keys, Eva?" the woman in the crimson armor asked her. "What are we going to find down the second shaft, Eva?"

A minute later Dr. Eva Hocks' sobs turned to screams, and then her screams died with her.

Bethany Anne wiped the blood off her mouth. "I fucking hate that shit, but if there was ever a bitch who deserved to provide me energy this tea-bagging self-centered fucktwat was the one."

Bethany Anne's hand dropped to her right leg, from which a sword extended. She grabbed the sword and cut through Dr. Hock's neck. Returning the sword to its sheath, she told the team, "Not taking a chance she can come back to life. Now, let's go get the keys. We need everyone." She walked back toward the operations room to get one of the keys from the dead operations manager.

"We have some nasty shit below, people."

CHAPTER TWENTY-FOUR

The hallway was silent when the woman in the crimson armor appeared. She stopped fifteen feet down it, and behind her the elevator doors opened.

"Would you stop doing that shit?" John bitched as he and Eric walked past her and continued down the hall. The elevator doors closed and went back up for the next group.

In ten minutes they had a number of people searching the level.

They found nothing and no one.

"Thoughts?" John asked.

"Bethany Anne?" Dan's voice came across the line.

"Yes?"

"Team Two has run into a few humans trying to escape. Two down, two captured."

"Thank you. We have any other holes they are trying to leave from?"

"So far, no."

"We have some shit ahead of us. According to the woman in charge of science, we have aliens genetically manipulating humans down here and many of them are ugly."

"Why are you going in personally?" Dan asked, "Why not just release the EI antipersonnel weapons?"

"Because," Bethany Anne replied and closed the comm. She popped her helmet latches and pulled the helmet off, then scratched her head. "Is it me, or do these things make your head itch?"

Outside, Dan swore under his breath.

Kael-ven turned to him. "She didn't answer the question, did she?" the alien asked.

"Yeah, she answered," Dan told him. "The answer was BBADWT."

Kael-Ven moved his shoulders in his version of a shrug.

Dan made a face. "Because Bethany Anne Doesn't Want To."

"Fucking shit," she griped. "If I could jump out of this armor, I could jump through the Etheric and…"

"NO!" six different voices yelled at her in unison.

"Yesss!" one Pricolici added a second late. Everyone in the group turned toward Peter, who smiled. "I'llll jjjooiinnn youuu!"

"Fuck it." Her eyes started to glow, her cheeks showing lines of red power as she pulled energy like crazy. Locking the helmet back on, she started walking down the hallway. The men fell in behind her, two by two.

They went down the hallway and went down five levels using the stairs.

On each leg her armor opened, and she grabbed the swords. The armor folded back in, hiding the sword compartments.

This time, though, she fed energy into the hilts of the swords and the blades glowed and elongated.

Jean had done wonders, and now her swords could channel Etheric energy.

She kicked open the sixth-level door and screamed, "Dress Rehearsal for *HELL*, boys!"

Ztopik stood behind the last cage, the one he refused to yet open. He wanted to see how each group of his mutants would function against these attackers.

He could feel their approach in his mind, and the sheer power of the female in front. Then they arrived on his level, and it was all he could do to pay attention to the slaughter.

"You're telling me," Eric asked, shooting something that was a cross between an ape and a female human, the deformed experiment's scream tearing through his soul. "These were all human at one point?"

"YES!" Bethany Anne yelled. "FUCKING SHIT!" She threw her two red, glowing swords into the air and kicked something running at her, which caved in its head and stopped it in its tracks. She grabbed the swords as they came back down and used her left sword to cut off the head.

Nathan and Peter stood to her left, ripping through the surge of mutants. The Yollin mercenaries to her right were beating the shit out of anything they could grab to save their ammunition.

She could hear the roars of the Pricolici as they ripped into genetic mutations that came from a truly twisted imagination.

"*WE HAVE ALIENS!*" one of the Yollins yelled, its voice suddenly cut off.

"SHIT!" Kiel's voice came over the line. "They have disintegrators!"

"Bitches, *TO ME!*" she yelled. More and more Queen's Guardians and Queen's Marines flooded into the huge cave, guns and growls everywhere as her men and women fought for their world, for their friends, and for their Queen.

The glow of the swords died when she pulled the energy back into herself and sheathed them. John, Eric, Scott, Darryl, and, with a roar of vengeance, Peter came tearing through the fighting. "I've got that motherfucking cunt, and he is going to *die!*" she spat, angry at the inhumanity of this alien's twisted experiments and the hell her people were in, having to kill those twisted into inhuman forms.

These beasts looked at them with very human eyes.

Bethany Anne's right hand went out palm forward and a glowing red orb developed. This time it didn't stop at six inches. In her anger, it continued to grow.

"Uh, boss?" John called, and Bethany Anne threw the ball.

The explosion occurred two-thirds of the way toward the clear, mental siren call of the alien. Toward the back of the massive cavern spread with the dead, the dying, and the burned, its energy continued through the air. Cages, some melting, were blasted out of the way.

The Queen Bitch and her protectors strode across the floor and destroyed anything that came remotely close to them. The few aliens that looked in their direction lost their heads when kinetic projectiles slammed into them.

It was mass carnage.

Bethany Anne and her team finally noticed a big-ass cage and the beast within.

"What the fuck is that?" Eric asked.

"Target practice." Bethany Anne threw a ball of Etheric energy. It streaked across the remaining distance and exploded against the bars, electric arcs racing all around the cage.

That wasn't so smart, a voice observed inside of their heads. *The*

Zhool'tai'ch is a very vicious beast, the best I have created. Interestingly, it wasn't made with any human DNA.

"Well, the bigger they are." John flipped his pistols up to ten. "Crank it up, Bitches."

Bethany Anne pointed at the fifteen-foot cross between a crocodile and an orangutan. "Kill that thing," she commanded.

The energy dissipated and the beast roared as it pushed open the cage door. It started running toward Bethany Anne.

Ztopik watched with interest. The female was calmly walking toward him, but the Zhool'tai'ch would certainly get to her first. She didn't have any obvious weapons, nor was she creating those glowing red balls of destruction.

His eyes flashed pink as the Zhool'tai'ch charged, and it went right through her when she disappeared and then reappeared. Enraged, it began to turn when those behind her started shooting it and massive chunks of flesh exploded from its body. It turned toward its tormentors.

The woman, however, kept coming toward him.

The alien spoke in her mind. *This would almost be amusing if you and your people had not just destroyed seventy years of my hard work!*

"Cry me a fucking river. You got a name, or should I just call you 'Shithead?'" she retorted.

"You may call me 'Ztopik' or 'Master!'" the alien exclaimed, and Bethany Anne's body froze.

Bethany Anne fought the mental command that stopped her in her tracks. The harder she fought, the more frozen her body became.

Bethany Anne, straining with all she had, started cursing violently as the alien snickered at the sub-level being in front of him.

"You see," Ztopik pulled out a disintegrator from the sleeve of his robe. "I might not be as physically impressive as you, but when you are a superior species, it is enough."

Ztopik felt another enter their conversation and his blood went cold.

Motherfucker, the alien voice snarled, **who said my friend lacked mental defenses?**

"Who are you?" Ztopik cried as immense pain slammed into his head, and his frail arms reached out to catch himself as his knees buckled.

My name is Thales of Miletus. I am Kurtherian, and you are my bitch!

Bethany Anne, released from Ztopik's mental hold, resumed walking toward him. Her left arm shot out and a two-inch red globe of power streaked across the cavern to blast away two aliens that had cornered a Wechselbalg and her Guardian Marine partner.

"FUCK, YEAH!" she heard her people scream and she grinned ferociously.

"Kurtherian?" Ztopik cried, the pain causing him to whisper.

Bethany Anne reached for her sword, but TOM stopped her.

Yes, he told Ztopik. **Kurtherian. My friend has a saying about reducing bad genetics after the birth, and I've decided she is *right*.**

"What?" Ztopik whispered, looking up into the flaming red eyes of the human.

Ztopik heard the woman's voice through his ears as the Kurtherian's voice slammed into his cranium.

"Die, you bastard!" was Bethany Anne's contribution.

TOM, Thales of Miletus, Kurtherian pilot lost on an alien world, broke through his own conditioning and reached deep into the alien's brain to find the link keeping him alive.

This is *my* friend, TOM whispered telepathically. ***No one* touches her mind without permission!**

Ztopik's eyes glazed and he died as his brain seized, then cratered from TOM's mental attack.

Bethany Anne turned around and viewed the carnage. At least seventeen of her people were on the ground.

As she put her helmet back on, she walked toward the middle of the large cave. The carcass of the Zhool'tai'ch, looking like hamburger, lay some twenty yards to her left.

They had some cleanup to do so she opened her palms, red balls starting to glow in her hands.

Let's do this. I got your back!

I never doubted it, TOM.

New York City, New York, USA

"We are in agreement?" The other three ambassadors nodded.

"The president is willing to make the call as soon as we have signatures," the United States Ambassador told Zhou.

Ambassador Zhou opened his briefcase, pulled out the document, and placed it on the table.

The document showed the signatures of many countries already, and the US ambassador's eyes widened in surprise. He picked up the document and read through the who's who of major and minor countries represented.

He failed to see Japan, Australia, or Germany on the document, but there was sufficient space to add them later.

He reached into his suit jacket and pulled out a pen. With a flourish, he signed the document on one of the top lines and put the pen back in his jacket. "Sorry." He pulled it back out and held it out to Ambassador Emeka. "Do you gentlemen need to sign as well?"

The other two ambassadors took their turns and signed the document before the US ambassador accepted the pen back. He moved it to the other coat pocket.

That pen was going to be worth money one day.

Unfortunately he didn't realize that it would be infamous,

known as the Pen of Destruction. It was true, some would say, that the pen did accomplish what the sword never could have.

"There is no time like the present to make the world's will known," Zhou told the US ambassador. "Here is the location of one of their ships presently over Japan."

"We can't fire a sub-nuke over Japan," the ambassador stated.

"True, but if they move east or west we have them," Zhou replied. The US ambassador nodded and reached out for the information the Chinese Ambassador had provided.

Japan

Captain Natalia Jakowski hugged Yuko and shook Akio's hand. "See you when we see you." She walked back into the *G'laxix Sphaea*. Her crewman closed up as she strode to the bridge and sat in the captain's chair.

It was her week to rotate into this ship, and she loved it.

Within a minute the sleek craft crested the tree line and started to break toward the west. She was headed toward Europe to drop off a couple of caches.

They were barely over the East China Sea when the alarms started squealing.

"We have inbound SLBM, Trident II D-5 on intercept," the *G'laxix Sphaea*'s EI reported.

"Implement defensive puck field. Seek and destroy!" Captain Jakowski snapped. Admiral Thomas had them run drills all the time, and being nuked was only one of them.

The holographic tank sprang into view in front of Natalia's seat. She pulled her hands apart and it zoomed out, showing the location of the submarine-launched ballistic missile.

"Defensive puck field in place. Calculate intercept of incoming missile at seventeen-point-four nautical miles."

Seconds later the EI spoke again. "Missile destroyed by

kinetic collision. No nuclear explosion, chance of radioactive residue calculated as likely."

"Fuck those assholes!" Natalia bit off the rest of her comment. "G'laxix Sphaea, cloak us."

"SIR!" the radar operator on the US Ohio-class submarine called. "We've lost the target."

The captain's sharp nod accepted the result.

He had followed his orders, may God have mercy on the souls who made that decision.

Bethany Anne and her team had exited the base after searching through it multiple times. What they could grab, they did.

The rest? Well, they planted devices to implode the caves.

>> **Bethany Anne.**<<

Yes, ADAM?

>>**The G'laxix Sphaea has been fired on by a nuclear missile over the East China Sea.**<<

WHAT! Those near Bethany Anne watched as her eyes started glowing. They quickly looked around and checked their tablets for news.

>>**The ship and all crew are well, but Captain Jakowski is asking if she should continue the operation or leave?**<<

Tell her we can do another run as necessary. Leave Earth. Tell my commanders I want a meeting ASAP.

Her eyes never dimmed during the whole trip to the QBS *ArchAngel.*

CHAPTER TWENTY-FIVE

QBBS _Meredith Reynolds_

The attractive South American reporter looked into her compact mirror and checked her makeup and hair. Putting the compact away, she smiled and nodded to her camerawoman.

"Ready, Giannini?" Sia asked her friend, who nodded. Sia moved the camera a little to the right and really looked at her friend. "We don't have to do this if you want to stay on Earth." She nodded behind her. "The last ship to Earth leaves in three days."

Giannini shook her head. "No, Sia. I've seen enough these last three years. I don't know what the Earth's path is, but my path—"

"Our path," Sia interrupted.

"Our path, my heart, is to go to the stars and report what we find out there." Giannini smiled. "I used to think that I needed to rise in the eyes of my bosses."

"And now?" Sia asked.

"Now, I need to rise in my own eyes, to do what all reporters should," Giannini answered. She straightened her shoulders and looked ready to start her commentary.

"OK," Sia asked, adjusting the camera so she could get Giannini's profile and the large park inside the *Meredith Reynolds* in the background. "What's that?"

"Report the truth, report on our government, and support the people," Giannini answered.

"Wow, big pants to wear," Sia's muffled voice replied. "What do you think Bethany Anne is going to say about you reporting on the government?"

Giannini smiled. "Who do you think gave me the pants to put on?"

Sia smiled. "You're on in three. Two. One…"

"Hello." Giannini spoke to the camera. "My name is Giannini Oviedo and I'm coming to you from the Mark Billingsly Memorial Park inside the QBBS *Meredith Reynolds*. This is our last report before the Etheric Empire's ships cross the line separating this solar system from the Yollins'…"

The president looked down at the piece of paper laying on his desk. A knife with the imprint of a vampire's skull on the hilt had been buried deeply into his desk to pin it in place. Neither had been there just three minutes ago when he stepped out to use the restroom.

He reached forward and grabbed the knife, having to lever it back and forth to yank it out.

He unfolded the paper and his lips compressed as he read the words.

There are two ways I can finish this war you started. You can try again and I will rain fire from heaven on your places of power, completely obliterating your ability to wage war, or you can Leave Us The Fuck Alone. If you choose option one, I will start at the top—just as easily as I put this knife in your desk.

And as I told the Chinese, there will be nothing left of your military

except machines blackened by fire and people praying for the souls of
your dead. You DO remember how that ended, don't you?

    Queen Bethany Anne, Etheric Empire
    The Queen Bitch.

Dulce, New Mexico, USA

Tanya drove the last twelve miles in the Jeep she had bought off Craigslist. These damned vehicles cost an arm and a leg, even fifteen years old.

She had shopped at the Goodwill back in Phoenix before purchasing the Jeep and driving out to Dulce. Given that she'd had no communication from Patrick, she had a good idea what must have happened to the base while she was making her way back from Europe.

She parked the car at an old gas station a mile from the front entrance to the base. Once communications had stopped, Tanya had started working hard to erase her back trail, making blind moves, randomly choosing a different city to fly to, and waiting a couple days before flying again.

Eventually arriving back in New Mexico.

She opened the Jeep's door and got out, reaching back for her backpack to make sure she looked like she was just an average hiker this afternoon.

Placing the aviator sunglasses on her face and the olive-green baseball cap on her head, she pulled her hair through the hole in the back and started walking the trail leading from behind the building into the trees.

An hour later, she stepped out from behind the tree she had used to study the building a couple of hundred yards away.

No one moved, and nothing looked like it had been disturbed in days.

. . .

QBBS *Meredith Reynolds*

>>**Bethany Anne, there is a female watching the Majestic 12 base.**<<

Bethany Anne stopped looking at the readiness reports and reached over to the fruit bowl to grab an apple. After cleaning it, she ordered, "Show me."

A video came up on the wall in her ready room as she bit into the fruit. She pointed with the hand that had the apple at the screen. "Hey, that looks like the chick in the MJ-12 images."

>>**There is a match on her jawline and mouth.**<<

"Call John and make sure he gets to watch this." She took another bite of the apple, her crunching filled the silence in the room.

Two minutes later there was a knock on her door.

"Come in," she called and tossed the apple core into the trash, the noise of the apple landing syncing with the door opening.

"Brought Jean with me," John announced and the two of them walked in, stepping toward Bethany Anne and looking at the wall to see what she was watching.

"*THAT BITCH!*" Jean shouted, pointing at the woman on the screen. "That's the fucking twatknuckle who was stalking our men!" She snorted in disgust.

"ADAM, are you recording this?" Bethany Anne asked.

"Yes," he responded.

"Good." Jean pulled out a chair beside Bethany Anne. "What are we about to do to the geriatric cuntquat?" she asked, sitting down.

"Not so much *us* doing something to her as her former friends." Bethany Anne reached into the bowl of fruit a second time. "I need some popcorn."

"Heard that!" Gabrielle called from the hall outside. "We got time?"

"Yeah," Bethany Anne called back. "Looks like she's studying the building to see if there's a trap."

Gabrielle came in carrying two bags of popcorn, a Coke, and three other beverages. "Well, there is one, right?"

"Yup," Bethany Anne agreed. "Lots of alien explosives all around the area."

Five minutes later, the room was crowded. All the Bitches were there, along with Peter, Nathan, Ecaterina, and little Christina Bethany Anne, who was coloring on the table with her back to the video. The little girl, now almost four, reached toward the fruit, growing a claw on her finger and stabbing an orange. She pulled it off her claw and her finger returned to normal again. She put it to the side and picked up the green crayon and started filling in the trees.

Frank and Barb arrived, with Lance and Patricia right behind them. Stephen and Jennifer were right behind them.

Jennifer asked what they were watching and Barb told her this was the bitch who had been stalking the guys during the camera shoot and who they had figured out was behind the ambush in Europe. "Oh," Jennifer responded. "So, we going to kill her?"

"Oh, hell, yeah," Cheryl Lynn called from in front of Scott. She was leaning back against her man, and his arms were around her. "Can't wait to see the pretty explosion."

"Hey, move over!" Bobcat called to the general laughter as he, William, and Marcus arrived. Those in the middle picked up chairs and handed them to the ones closer to the door to store in the hallway.

"ADAM, duplicate this image on the ceiling as well as the other walls," Bethany Anne directed. "Except the one in front of Christina. Don't want anyone not able to see the ending to the movie."

Fifteen minutes later, the general conversation in the room quieted down to where the only noise was little Christina's coloring.

The woman started walking toward the building. When she

reached it she adjusted her backpack, then knocked on the door and called out. She stood there for a minute before trying the open door.

The viewpoint in the video rapidly ascended to at least three hundred feet higher in the air and another two hundred north.

Everyone in the room cheered and shouted with joy as the building exploded, raining shrapnel down for almost forty-five seconds.

"Got you, bitch!" Bethany Anne exclaimed.

"Now, that," Lance stated smugly, "was good television!"

Barb asked with exasperation, "Frank, sweetheart, why are you writing this down?"

"It ends my book!" His voice was clearly heard by all in the room as he told his wife, "It's perfect!"

QBS _ArchAngel_

Bethany Anne looked at the Yollin. "Are you sure about this, Kael-ven? You can't reverse this decision and I don't want you to regret making it."

"There will be no regret for my choice, Queen Bethany Anne. I have spoken to my people, and we are in agreement."

"Even Scientist Royleen?" she asked, a smile teasing her lips.

"Yes, even the ever-hardheaded Royleen sees the truth now."

Bethany Anne pursed her lips. "You'll have to allow me access to your thoughts. If it were only me I would be okay, but for me to accept this offer, I have to confirm for the sake of my people."

Captain Kael-ven T'chmon nodded and lowered his head, and Bethany Anne placed her hands on both sides of it. While not strictly required for her to read his thoughts, it helped her with the alien minds.

Tell me when you have his thoughts, TOM.

I'm in. Hold on a moment, TOM replied.

Seconds later he came back with, **He is being forthright, Bethany Anne.**

She pulled her hands off the Yollin. "Stand up, Captain Kael-ven T'chmon." She chewed the inside of her cheek. "You are an anomaly. I would like to know what changed your people's minds?"

His large mandibles opened wide a moment before closing. "We are requesting your help, so this is not subjugation."

"No?" she asked.

"No," he told her. "It is a revolution."

FINIS

NEVER SUBMIT

The Story Continues with book 15, *Never Submit*, available at Amazon and through Kindle Unlimited.

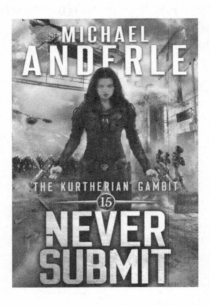

Available now at Amazon and on Kindle Unlimited

AUTHOR NOTES

THIS IS IT!

One Year Old A Few Days Ago.
Written November 11, 2016

As always, can I say with a HUGE amount of appreciation how much it means to me that you not only read this book, but you are reading these notes as well.?

Just one year and nine days ago I released the first book of The Kurtherian Gambit series, titled *Death Becomes Her*. Since that time this series has taken off to become a sleeper hit. I'm probably one of the most successful authors no one has heard about, because of fans who love not just the first book, but ALL the books.

I say "sleeper" because to date there have been a total of 11,019 of Book 01 sold, and 4,880,000 pages read (Kindle Unlimited). That would (based on 384 pages KENP V 2.0) be about another 12,708 full books read. Now, I know the total is higher (because books can be read, but author notes aren't etc.) but it does mean that at a minimum, the first book has been sold (read) a total of 23,727 times.

So, all of my success comes from approximately 25,000 readers. Readers who are then going on to read the REST of the books. Enough that as of last night (According to Amazon) I am the #172 top selling author on their store.

172.

There are over 200,000 authors minimum on Amazon. My original goal was just (sometime around end of November / Beginning of December 2015) to be in the top 2,000 authors on Amazon. Thanks to *YOU* and your sharing of the stories with friends, family, strangers in stores (this is literal, not figurative) I have been amazed to be counted in the top 500 authors on all of Amazon since July of this year!

That's freaking *UNBELIEVABLE.*

Just rocking our little story about Bethany Anne and her people and those around her has been life-changing for me and over a thousand other indie authors who joined the 20Books-To50k group that came out of my success.

Trying to give back to other authors.

I could share stories how that group of authors, helping each other, support them getting their own stories out and how YOU, my readers, help them make it happen!

Just this week, readers of the snippets took a book that was listed as the 92,000th ranked book (based on sales) on Amazon and within 24 hours, moved it up to under 10,000 for two days. I didn't know it at the time, but the author I was supporting (Boyd Craven III) was coming back from a sudden trip to check on his father who had fallen very sick and concerns were heavy about his health…

The other author of the book the fans pushed up? His father, Boyd Craven Jr.

His father recovered, thankfully. But it was a sobering feeling that we helped make a good thing happen in the life of someone who could use another good thing to occur at that time.

What's going on with Audio?

For those who love Audiobooks, I have some great news. I am

this close (see two fingers pinched close together) to finding a narrator.

I hope. *Lord in Heaven PLEASE I hope.* I've had 19 auditions so far, and 17 have been (some after MUCH review) put in the 'no' group.

Two are left and I have one request out to a huge name to see if she has any interest. The problem? Well, it's hard to handle the size of these stories without massive talent.

She (and it will be a lady I pick) needs to be able to read the story in an engrossing way, do Bethany Anne well and men in a way that works. It's a freaking HUGE challenge and I was pretty upfront about the issues.

Think about it. One actress will be handling Bethany Anne, TOM and ADAM all in one head. Then, add in the Bitches, Gabrielle, Tabitha, Frank, Lance, Nathan etc. etc. ;-)

But however long it takes, it will be worth it because I'm setting aside the money to make the first seven books happen. I refuse to "Do one book to see if it sells" model and leave fans hanging.

So I'm looking for one of the best, and I'll pay her for her talent and skills because I really, really want Bethany Anne and the Bitches to come alive.

What's a Yollin look like?

So, a fan on Facebook asked about what Yollins looked like (sorry, I looked but couldn't find the fan's name that asked). Now, that was an awesome question, and the only problem was the artist I used for my Bethany Anne stuff (Andrew Dobell) doesn't draw creatures/aliens. My artist that is working on the covers and spaceships (Jeff Brown) doesn't do a lot of creature/alien work either.

Where the hell was I going to find an artist that would work with me (who was dependable)? I asked Jeff Brown if he knew anyone and he suggested Eric Quigley.

I looked at his artwork, thinking...I want him! Now, if I can just afford him.

So far (audio will easily beat this in the near future, but right now) nothing costs me near as much as all the artwork and covers I am doing.

I'm spending enough to buy a small car on this stuff, so I needed a creature artist that I could afford, as well as who would do an amazing job.

So, check out the two Yollin art pieces in the back of this book (I hope you can all see them! Some are in color, to I will be placing the pieces up on my website in the coming week for everyone to enjoy, even the black-and-white kindle fans). He'll be doing Captain Kael-Ven next.

Remember, my website is http://www.kurtherianbooks.com.

I think Eric is going to do smashingly on the aliens for the last arc in The Kurtherian Gambit and allow us to better visualize these beings.

In the future, fans willing, I'm going to put out a Kurtherian Gambit e-Book on the artwork and show the different stuff we have all worked on, and give you a history of how one indie author has spent thousands and thousands on art for his series.

By the time I'm done with twenty-one books (and others) I'll have easily spent over $20,000 on artwork alone. I want this stuff as much as fans seem to want to see it, so together I think we can make some COOL art and I look forward to more of you asking questions like... *"What's a Yollin look like?"*

;-)

So, where are we going?

The Kurtherian Gambit's scope is huge. I've explained before (Here? Don't remember) that I wanted to have a world I could play in and do a lot with. I wanted to play with vampires and aliens and Military Sci-Fi and worlds and spaceships (oh my!) and AIs and so on and so on.

And due to the huge social support of fans, especially on the

FB ads and their own links and interactions. I get to do that. It's a huge blessing.

And it is getting bigger.

With the next release for Bethany Anne, *Never Submit*, we will be in another solar system, having left Earth behind and to their own devices. What happens to them? What happened, some will ask, between books 13 and 14 (the three years)?

Well, I'm happy you asked!

In order to produce additional insights into these events, some of the authors I've befriended on 20BooksTo50k have agreed to work in collaborative efforts to enhance the Kurtherian Universe. In awesome ways.

These aren't Frank Kurns 15-20k words books. These are true books and series with additional characters. One with a character you have seen before (Terry "TH to his Friend" Walton) and completely new vampires who have little understanding of what happened when TQB was part of the world, but exist when Michael comes back in The Dark Messiah (12.25.2016).

I'll give you more info after the author notes, but we have TS (Scott) Paul doing a YA series w/ the children of the Etheric Empire set during the 3 years between books 13 and 14. Justin Sloan and his vampire Valerie who leaves behind Europe in the future to protect New York City State from her brother Donovan (see snippet at end of book). Finally, we have Craig Martelle, who is taking TH and showing us what happened to Earth after Bethany Anne left and how this man was affected, and then learns to forgive himself and become the protector that was always inside of him.

With a vengeance.

All leading up to The Dark Messiah Series and Michael's return. Michael has a promise to fulfill, and Death isn't going to keep him from doing it.

Because his Honor requires it.

By the end of 2017 I will have released nine (9) more books.

Six (6) in The Kurtherian Gambit (Bethany Anne) series (through book 20) and three (3) in the Second Dark Ages (Michael) series.

I will be collaborating on another eleven (11) (minimum) books from these authors and perhaps a couple more (J.L. Hendricks for Romance stories between books 13 and 14). I am finishing one with Paul C. Middleton for The Boris Chronicles and he will release a fourth second quarter 2017.

So stay with us, if you will, as we bring Justice, Friendship and all around BadAssery to stories and to each other as the Indie Publishing Outlaw pulls out his Jean Dukes Specials and tips his hat up with the barrel.

Telling those who believe they know best about what readers want, "You sure about that? Because if you aren't, why don't you take a sit right where you are at and let us tell you a new story in The Kurtherian Universe."

As we move from 25,000 fans to 100,000 and beyond. Kicking Ass and Taking Names all along the way!

THANK YOU ALL!
Michael Anderle

BOOKS BY MICHAEL ANDERLE

Sign up for the LMBPN email list to be notified of new releases and special deals!

https://lmbpn.com/email/

For a complete list of books by Michael Anderle, please visit:

www.lmbpn.com/ma-books/

CONNECT WITH THE AUTHOR

Connect with Michael Anderle

Website: http://lmbpn.com

Email List: https://michael.beehiiv.com/

https://www.facebook.com/LMBPNPublishing

https://twitter.com/MichaelAnderle

https://www.instagram.com/lmbpn_publishing/

https://www.bookbub.com/authors/michael-anderle

Made in the USA
Las Vegas, NV
04 June 2024

90698414R00177